the **information** store

📞 01603 773114
email: tis@ccn.ac.uk

21 DAY LOAN ITEM

CITY
COLLEGE
NORWICH

NEW PENGUIN SHAKESPEARE

GENERAL EDITOR: T. J. B. SPENCER

ASSOCIATE EDITOR: STANLEY WELLS

WILLIAM SHAKESPEARE

*

THE MERCHANT
OF VENICE

EDITED BY
W. MOELWYN MERCHANT

PENGUIN BOOKS

PENGUIN BOOKS

Published by the Penguin Group
Penguin Books Ltd, 27 Wrights Lane, London W8 5TZ, England
Penguin Books USA Inc., 375 Hudson Street, New York, New York 10014, USA
Penguin Books Australia Ltd, Ringwood, Victoria, Australia
Penguin Books Canada Ltd, 10 Alcorn Avenue, Toronto, Ontario, Canada M4V 3B2
Penguin Books (NZ) Ltd, 182–190 Wairau Road, Auckland 10, New Zealand

Penguin Books Ltd, Registered Offices: Harmondsworth, Middlesex, England

This edition first published in Penguin Books 1967
29 30 28

This edition copyright © Penguin Books, 1967
Introduction and notes copyright © W. Moelwyn Merchant, 1967
All rights reserved

Printed in England by Clays Ltd, St Ives plc
Set in Monotype Ehrhardt

CONTENTS

INTRODUCTION

The Merchant of Venice is a fairy tale. There is no more reality in Shylock's bond and the Lord of Belmont's will than in Jack and the Beanstalk.

> H. Granville-Barker, *Prefaces to Shakespeare*, 4 (1930)

THAT *is* a way of looking at it, of reading it, or of settling oneself to enjoy a performance in the theatre. But somehow it flatly contradicts our deepest intuitions concerning this strange and complex play. At one level of response *The Merchant of Venice* will appear to be a romantic weaving of tales without logic; yet it would be a superficial reading, a perfunctory performance, which remained at that level. Portia's father may have denied some of our concerns for a lover's freedom of choice in his beloved; the conditions of Shylock's bond may have violated most known legal codes; but the coherence of the play, the movement of the dramatic poetry, takes us beyond these doubts and cavillings. We are convinced of the essential sanity of the casket-test for Portia's suitors; we fear Shylock's bond and anticipate tragedy, however 'merry' its terms may be; we accept the seriousness and technical gravity of the trial scene, whatever doubts the juristic side of our minds may plead; we respond gravely to the nature of usury and to the contrasts of charity, compassion, and equity; the dignity and grotesquerie in Shylock maintain a portrait of the Jew through which we assent today to the dark problems of 'race'. These are no fairy-tale matters, though the fairy-tale tone is frequently there.

The reader or spectator poised between fantasy and reality when confronted with a play by Shakespeare is no rare thing. *A Midsummer Night's Dream* is a fairy-tale, but the dark and even sinister possibilities that lie in the woodland confusions become the measure of a secure, radiant conclusion, in which Bottom's dream is revealed as a rare vision and the reunited lovers grow to an understanding 'of great constancy'. It is usually unsafe to mistake Shakespeare's lightness of touch for levity, or assume that an illogical fantasy, as early as *The Merchant of Venice* or as late as *The Tempest*, is a mere tale, a moment of relaxation.

We attempt to date the play by matters of very precise reality: the entry in the Stationers' Register of 22 July 1598, of 'a booke of the Marchaunt of Venyce, or otherwise called the Jewe of Venyce'; a reference in Francis Meres's *Palladis Tamia* (1598) in which '*Shakespeare* among the English is the most excellent in both kinds [Comedy and Tragedy] for the stage: for Comedy witness his ... Merchant of Venice'; by its critical relation to Marlowe's *The Jew of Malta* (Stationers' Register, 17 May 1594) and its relation in turn to Roderigo Lopez, a Portuguese Jew who was executed in June 1594 for an alleged attempt to poison the Queen and Don Antonio, pretender to the throne of Portugal. To become even more precisely particular, Salerio's reference, early in the first scene, to 'my wealthy Andrew docked in sand' has been generally accepted as a reference to the Spanish vessel, *St Andrew*, captured at the Cadiz expedition of 1596 and afterwards a notable vessel in Queen Elizabeth's command; this may well be so (and assists in dating the play), but an attractive additional reference may be found in the name of the formidable Genoese naval commander and *condottiere* Andrea Doria

(1466–1560), who helped reduce the menace of the Turkish 'salt-water thieves' in the western Mediterranean – Shylock's 'pirates'. This is a not unlikely possibility by analogy with the term 'Andrew' used of a sword, from the name of the swordsmith Andrea Ferrara.

From such a mosaic of small details, in themselves insignificant, the dating and context of the play may be roughly determined: probably between 1596 and 1598.

How important is it to determine this dated context, the 'contemporary relevance', 'contemporary' that is to say for Shakespeare, not for ourselves? When we read or watch *Love's Labour's Lost* we resign ourselves to missing a number of private topicalities and witticisms which seem to be assumed in the text, while enjoying both Shakespeare's and our own attitude to 'academic' grace and learning; we observe *Richard II* on regality and regicide, while not being overburdened with the thought that in Shakespeare's day it was assumed to have been 'deliberately composed as a political allegory, with the purpose of warning Elizabeth I of her possible fate if she encouraged flatterers and permitted unjust taxation and monopolies'. Apart from our momentary interest in local Elizabethan meanings or references, it is clear that *The Merchant of Venice* is much preoccupied with two matters of Elizabethan concern: Jewry and usury. So pervasive are these two questions that it is dangerously possible to assume that the play is 'about' race and greed; indeed, when a director tries to give edge and point to a new reading of the play in the theatre, it is all too easy to explore these Elizabethan aspects of the play in terms which refer to our present concern with racial and economic conflict. The greater, then, is our obligation to be clear about the intellectual and emotional limits within which Shakespeare could have handled these questions.

They are of course not the same question, though Jews

9

and usurers were too frequently identified. It is popularly assumed that the Elizabethan attitude to Jewry was one of uniform hostility and that the execration of Lopez was wholly characteristic of the Christian rejection of all 'Jews, Turks, Infidels, and Heretics' (see the note to I.3.108). This is in many respects a false assumption. Raphael Holinshed, chronicling the coronation of Richard I in 1189, indicates an aspect of the medieval temper in the opening description (*History of England*, 1577, p. 477):

> *Upon this day of King Richard's coronation, the Jews that dwelt in London and in other parts of the realm, being there assembled, had but sorry hap as it chanced, for they meaning to honour the same coronation with their presence, and to present to the King some honourable gift . . . King Richard, of a zealous mind to Christ's religion, abhorring their nation (and doubting some sorcery by them to be practised), commanded that they should not come within the church when he should receive the crown, nor within the palace whilst he was at dinner.*

A riot broke out against the Jews, which Holinshed describes in tones of total condemnation:

> *The King being advertised of this riotous attempt of the outrageous people . . . the rude sort of those that were about to spoil, rob, and sack the houses and shops of the Jews. . . . This wode* [mad] *rage of the furious and disordered people continued from the middle of the one day till two of the clock on the other, the commons all that while never ceasing their fury against that nation, but still killing them as they met with any of them, in most horrible, rash, and unreasonable manner.*

Holinshed's unambiguous attitude is quite consciously adopted, for he goes on to admit that the 'transgressors' were not punished, since the greater number of Richard's subjects hated the Jews for their 'obstinate frowardness', though the king halted the persecution, 'and so they were restored to peace after they had sustained infinite damage'. This is the temper in which it is possible to read *The Jew of Malta* and *The Merchant of Venice*. Marlowe's 'savage farce' (T. S. Eliot's valuable suggestion) depicts a Machiavellian Jew, but he is rarely mean in his villainy and he opens with a fine and dignified wit in his rejection of mere money as he reckons his wealth:

> *Here have I pursed their paltry silverlings.*
> *Fie, what a trouble 'tis to count this trash!*

He admires rather

> *The wealthy Moor, that in his eastern rocks*
> *Without control can pick his riches up ...*
> *Bags of fiery opals, sapphires, amethysts,*
> *Jacinths, hard topaz, grass-green emeralds,*
> *Beauteous rubies, sparkling diamonds ...*

These 'seld-seen costly stones' are the true and noble means of exchange for 'men of judgement' –

> *And as their wealth increaseth, so inclose*
> *Infinite riches in a little room.*

In that line, expressing a search for quintessential wealth with beauty, the Jew is cast in no ignoble role.

The treatment of usury, trade, debt, and interest is still more ambiguous, for Antonio and Shylock live in worlds removed from each other. Antonio lives by trade; his 'increase', which Shylock is able to denigrate as 'ventures ... squandered abroad', is seen even by his friends to be at the mercy of storms and 'merchant-marring rocks'. Antonio exacts no interest, while Shylock thrives by no other means. Yet the ironies of the play depend on the mutual contempt of both Gentile and Jew for each other's way of 'thrift'. And the irony is redoubled, since each is self-justified and condemns the other on sound theological grounds. Shylock's meditative pride on his descent from Abraham, sharing his ancestry with Jacob 'The third possessor', is mingled with an ironic pleasure both in Jacob's crafty deceit of his father, under Rebeccah's tuition (see note to I.3.68–71) and his stratagem over the breeding of Laban's sheep (see note to I.3.75–85). The latter passage is an argument in oblique justification of interest or usury, but the crux comes at Antonio's questioning of the analogy between sheep and gold:

ANTONIO

   This was a venture, sir, that Jacob served for,
   A thing not in his power to bring to pass,
   But swayed and fashioned by the hand of heaven.
   Was this inserted to make interest good?
   Or is your gold and silver ewes and rams?

SHYLOCK

   I cannot tell, I make it breed as fast.

To this claim, some forty lines later, Antonio makes tacit rejoinder in the phrase, 'A breed of *barren* metal'. These counter-assumptions, that metal and coin can or cannot reproduce themselves like organic creatures, have an ancient verbal lineage. The Greek and Latin background is summarized by Julius Paulus, writing at the beginning of the third century A.D.:

   Usury, usurers and the law concerning loans are called 'fenebris' from the word 'fetus', since money on loan gives birth to money: for the same reason the Greeks call this process TÓKOS [a word that could carry the diverse senses of childbirth, offspring of animals or men and (metaphorically, in both Plato and Aristophanes) interest on a loan].

Antonio adopts the astringent rule that usury may not be levied ('I do never use it'). Shylock, who would be restrained by Deuteronomic law from exacting usury from a fellow-Jew, is under no such obligation in financial dealings with a Gentile (just as a Gentile within the Jewish community could claim no right to participate in the seventh-year remission of debts known as the Jubilee). This confrontation of principles represented by Shylock and Antonio, an argument on the moral justification or condemnation of usury, proceeds without the bland irony with which the medieval mind faced the hard facts of trade in a sinful world. This tone is most adequately conveyed by the fourteenth-century writer Benvenuto da Imola:

Qui facit usuram vadit ad infernum; qui non facit ad inopiam. [*He who takes usury goes to hell; he who does not, to the workhouse.*]

The irony of *The Merchant of Venice* is quite different; if Antonio rejects interest with something of the moral scorn of a Sir Thomas Wilson, whose *Discourse upon Usury* (1572) was a classic source of invective, his Christian friends in Venice have no hesitation in living upon 'excess'. Indeed sixteenth-century Venice was notable for its corruption through the covetous pursuit of trade and 'venture'. On the other side Shylock proceeds on the assumption, morally grounded, that interest on money-lending is legitimate thrift (there being no Jews with whom his financial dealings would be bounded by the prohibitions of Deuteronomy; for Tubal, 'a wealthy Hebrew of my tribe', could help him out in a crisis, presumably without the usury which Shylock could demand of his Gentile debtors).

Shakespeare's Venice, then, is nicely and justly poised between Christians on the one hand whose acquisitive practice by no means squares with their many protestations against usury, and Jews on the other whose disenchanted commercial dealings rest on the double pillars of expediency and Levitical Law. It is useful to have a background of Elizabethan moral writing on economic matters as a foil to the dramatists' constant reprehension of usury and to estimate the social conservatism of certain dramatists, notably Jonson and Shakespeare, in their attitude towards an emerging 'capitalist society'. But *The Merchant of Venice* bears not the least resemblance to a pamphlet on usury, despite the active polemics in the background. Shakespeare rarely 'takes sides' and it is certainly rash to assume that he here takes an unambiguous stand 'for' Antonio and 'against' Shylock – our moral judgement, in reading or watching the play, is far more delicately poised than this, our personal sympathies and our social alertness constantly adjusting themselves in a process of nice critical casuistry. We cannot even be sure that Shakespeare takes up a consistent attitude towards 'cormorant usury' and we may set the implications of 'A breed of barren metal' in this play (I.3.131) against an analogous passage in *Twelfth Night*, when Feste has successfully begged a piece of money from Viola (III.1.47–8):

FESTE *Would not a pair of these have bred, sir?*
VIOLA *Yes, being kept together and put to use.*

Here, in the nicely turned verbal play, 'bred – use – [usury]', Viola comes delicately near to Shylock's argument from the increase of Laban's sheep. And certainly, judging from his comedies as a whole, Shakespeare makes no simple or innocent gesture of assent towards any of the three main ways to wealth in his day – the land, foreign trade, or financial exchange. There is a certain detached irony in *As You Like It* as it contemplates the pastoral life, and *The Merchant of Venice* preserves a similar detachment in its view of trade and of dealings in money as a commodity. If, in Antonio's view, usury is reprehensible, Shylock observes with contempt Antonio's irresponsible 'ventures squandered abroad' in foreign trade; for Antonio's sober activities were necessarily linked to those of that other prodigal gambler, Bassanio, whose vast expenditure on wooing is laid out as a venture to win a 'golden fleece', Portia's fair person and wealth.

We may judge the quality of this dramatic detachment by considering a quotation from an equally conservative dramatist. In a terse passage in the first scene of *Volpone*, Ben Jonson summarizes the ways to wealth:

> *I glory*
> *More in the cunning purchase of my wealth*
> *Than in the glad possession, since I gain*
> *No common way; I use no trade, no venture;*
> *I wound no earth with ploughshares, I fat no beasts*
> *To feed the shambles; have no mills for iron,*
> *Oil, corn, or men, to grind them into powder;*
> *I blow no subtle glass, expose no ships*
> *To threat'nings of the furrow-faced sea;*
> *I turn no moneys in the public bank,*
> *No usure private.*

Each way of gain is reviewed in turn: 'trade', 'the earth', 'usure' – and each is placed and dismissed, first together, in the phrase 'no common way', and then successively; for trade is linked (for Volpone as for Shylock) with 'venture' and the threatenings of the sea; the earth is 'wounded' as it produces grain or supports beasts; banks and 'usure private' are equally contemned as the 'turning of moneys'. Shakespeare's purpose in *The Merchant of Venice* includes no such thoroughgoing and dismissive satire, but ironic judgement is suspended as deftly over the decadent acquisitiveness of the Venetians as it is brought to bear on the greed of Shylock and Tubal. *The Merchant of Venice* was played and first printed between the publication of Wilson's *Discourse upon Usury* in 1572 and Bacon's essay *Of Usury* in 1625; to the former, usurers are 'greedy cormorant wolves'; for the latter, 'to speak of abolishing usury is idle . . . it is better to mitigate usury by declaration than to suffer it to rage by connivance'. Shakespeare's moral tone is higher than this, employing neither the indignation of Wilson nor the more convenient expediency of Bacon. Nonetheless, in the clarity with which both usurer and legitimate trader are seen, Venice is depicted in decline, as we now see her, from our more historical perspective, ceding primacy among the bourses of Europe to Frankfurt and Antwerp.

*

The sources of Shakespeare's plays are far less interesting than his creative manipulation of them. For the Bond and Casket themes in *The Merchant of Venice* we may trace a long lineage, and though some investigation of sources can reveal areas of considerable dullness, the hinterland to this play has some fascinating by-ways. It is at this point that we most clearly enter Granville-Barker's realm of fairy-tale, though the most immediate 'source' must be assumed to be *The Jew of Malta* and the impetus it gave Shakespeare in the exploration of the relationships between an alien and a settled society. Barabas and Abigail, the Jewish father and daughter in Marlowe's play, are the complements rather than the parallels to Shylock and Jessica. Barabas is urbane, witty, of majestic greed and grotesque invention; the motive power of his religious conflict with the authorities of Malta is hatred of Christianity rather than a positive adherence to Jewry. Shylock is a Jewish puritan, with little of Barabas's sophistication; his faith, though embittered by persecution, has a positive prophetic quality, strengthened by supernatural sanctions. We may see this profound disparity in two asides: in Barabas's cynical loan to his Christian acquaintance of a commentary on the Maccabees (II.3.160) and Shylock's savouring of his scriptural references to Jacob and Laban, or his pointedly informed references to Christian scriptures ('your prophet the Nazarite'; see the note to I.3.32). The two daughters also are wholly opposed in quality. Jessica is Lorenzo's gentle 'infidel', stealing easily and lucratively into a casually Christian alliance; Abigail on the other hand takes at least temporary refuge in a convent from the bizarre pressures of her father's intrigues.

Behind the immediate influence of Marlowe's play lie the more precise sources of *The Merchant of Venice*, the long traditions of the Bond of Flesh and the Casket Choice, in some of the versions anticipating Shakespeare's union of the two themes. Shylock's 'merry bond' has sources in both fantasy and legal fact. In Eastern and Western tales we frequently find a surety in the form of a contract to give up a portion of the debtor's living flesh. Some versions are as old as the Indian compilation, the *Mahābhārata* (extending between 500 and 200 B.C.), which contains the legend of the noble king Usinara who gave up his flesh to save a dove from a falcon, the two birds at the conclusion of the tale revealing themselves to be the gods Indra and Agni. Myths and legends of this kind, including a fleshbond, were gathered together from many sources to eke out the biblical narrative in the fourteenth-century poem, *Cursor Mundi*. In another compilation, the *Gesta Romanorum*, the bond theme was for the first time linked to a tale of wooing. Here the debt incurred is a hundred florins and Portia's predecessor in the trial scene uses similar arguments to hers:

> '*what profit is it to thee that this knight, that standeth here ready to the doom, be slain? It were better to thee to have money than to have him slain.*' '*Thou speakest all in vain,*' quoth the merchant, '*for without doubt I will have the law.*'

The 'damsel' delivers him his strict legal judgement, with the same outcome as in Shakespeare's trial scene:

> '*Thou shalt not have one penny; for afore all this company I proferred to thee all that I might, and thou forsook it, and saidest with a loud voice, I shall have my covenant; and therefore do thy best with him, but look that thou shed no blood.*'

This is from a fifteenth-century manuscript giving a version of the story apparently not printed in Shakespeare's time, though other stories, including that of the caskets, were printed in translation by Wynkyn de Worde and later revised by Richard Robinson in 1577 and 1595 in a form probably known to Shakespeare.

The next probable source of the play to be considered is Ser Giovanni Fiorentino's *Il Pecorone* (1558), of which however there is no known English translation of Shakespeare's day, a matter of little consequence, for if he had no Italian, translations and versions of innumerable Italian works circulated orally and in manuscript in the circle of his friends. Ser Giovanni's tale contains a strangely sinister version of the wooing, a very full version of the Bond, and closes with the incident of the ring (see the version by

T. J. B. Spencer in *Elizabethan Love Stories*, Penguin
Shakespeare Library, 1967).

In English there appears to be a probable source in
Anthony Munday's *Zelauto*, published in 1580. In the
third part of these romantic stories we find 'The amorous
life of Strabino a scholar, the brave behaviour of Rodolfo
a martial gentleman, and the right reward of Signor
Truculento a usurer'. It will be seen that there is a distinct
flavour of the morality in the names and descriptions of the
characters, but some of the passages approach the temper
and even the words of *The Merchant of Venice*; first the
bond:

> *Well (quoth Truculento) this is the bond: if by the first
> day of the month ensuing the whole sum be not restored,
> each of your lands shall stand to the endamagement, besides
> the loss of both your right eyes. Are you content to stand to
> this bargain?*

In the final event the quibble is identical; to Truculento's
demand, 'I crave justice to be uprightly used, and I crave
no more, wherefore I will have it', Cornelia (Munday's
Portia) gives her learned opinion:

> *Receive the ransom you so much require, and take both
> their eyes. So shall the matter be ended. But thus much . . .
> I give you in charge . . . if in pulling forth their eyes, you
> diminish the least quantity of blood out of their heads . . .
> you shall stand to the loss of both your own eyes.*

The ballad of *Gernutus* is more questionable, for we have no
certainty that this tale of 'a Jew who, lending to a merchant
a hundred crowns, would have a pound of his flesh' was
extant in Shakespeare's day; in any event the doggerel
verse adds nothing to our understanding of Shakespeare.

Nor are we much the gainers from the speculations concerning a lost play, *The Jew*, described by Stephen Gosson in 1579 as a representation of 'the greediness of worldly choosers, and bloody minds of usurers', though the quality of this language is itself in distinct contrast with the temper of Shakespeare's play.

All these sources in fiction are given a possible substratum of fact by Elizabethan recollections of the Twelve Tables, a codification of Roman Civil Law dating back to the fifth century B.C. By the provisions of these Tables (though probably never enforced) a defaulting debtor's body could be divided among his creditors – but at this point we enter a subject, the intricacies of law, which greatly preoccupied Shakespeare, not least in *The Merchant of Venice*.

*

'But if it is a case beyond any law?' Oliver said. 'There is no case beyond the law,' the Chief Justice answered. 'We may mistake in the ruling, we may be deceived by outward things and cunning talk, but there is no dispute between men which cannot be resolved in equity. And in its nature equity is from those between whom it exists: it is passion acting in lucidity.'

Charles Williams, *Many Dimensions* (1931)

Justice without mercy were extreme injury and pity without equity plain partiality; and that it is as great tyranny not to mitigate laws as iniquity to break them.

John Lyly, *Euphues: The Anatomy of Wit* (1579)

The Merchant of Venice, and the fourth Act in particular, is Shakespeare's most elaborate statement of the relation of positive law to equity* in the dealings of man with man.

* 'Equity' is a highly ambiguous term. At its most general it is the quality of 'equitable dealing' between men or nations, governed by the principles of natural law 'written in the hearts of men'. At its

Though he made elsewhere, in *Measure for Measure*, in *Hamlet*, in many of the *Sonnets*, in *King Lear*, and in *The Winter's Tale*, pointed and mature references on the subject of law, the trial scene here focuses more aspects of the matter than any other dramatist or poet succeeded in uniting in one work. Indeed, it is remarkable that this relatively early play foreshadowed so many of the complex legal considerations which are so prominent in later, more mature plays: the personal factors in an apparently neutral matter of law, in *Measure for Measure*; the conflict of two systems of thought, of revenge and of charity within the law, in *Hamlet*; of the involvement of the whole natural order in the process of law, in *King Lear*.

It is probably best to begin with 'law' at its most fantastic, the sinister ground-bass of the apparently 'merry bond'. The stages in its dramatic exposition are clear. It begins at the level of jest, with even here an undertone of foreboding, both in the sardonic 'kindness' and in Bassanio's protest (I.3.141–51):

SHYLOCK
  Go with me to a notary, seal me there
  Your single bond, and, in a merry sport,
  If you repay me not on such a day . . .

ANTONIO
  Content, in faith. I'll seal to such a bond
  And say there is much kindness in the Jew.

BASSANIO
  You shall not seal to such a bond for me. . . .

---

narrowest it implies 'equity jurisdiction' in the Chancery Courts, and is therefore capable of mitigating the rigours of a Common Law action. Already, however, by Shakespeare's day this latter sense of equity was beginning to lose its flexible application of 'natural law' principles and tended, like the Common Law, to be bound by precedent.

Shylock's intention is soon given religious sanctions (III.1.115–19, and see note):

> Go, Tubal, fee me an officer . . . I will have the heart of him if he forfeit . . . Go, Tubal, and meet me at our synagogue. . . .

which is made explicit in his contemptuous rejection of Antonio's personal plea after his arrest (III.3.4–5):

> I'll have my bond! Speak not against my bond!
> I have sworn an oath that I will have my bond.

This is in turn repeated and sharpened at the trial (IV.1. 35–7):

> I have possessed your grace of what I purpose,
> And by our holy Sabbath have I sworn
> To have the due and forfeit of my bond. . . .

– an avenging tone which Victor Hugo described as 'consecrated . . . sacerdotal'.

The whole legal structure of the play is, of course, fallacious. No system of law permits a man to place his own person in jeopardy, for a bond like Antonio's is 'against public policy' and 'contrary to good morals'. Moreover Portia discovers a statute of no obscure import which would, from the proposal of such a bond, have rendered its terms invalid. Nor are these the only objections to the course of justice as it is demonstrated in the trial scene. The dramatic structure of the fourth Act assumes a relationship between Shylock and Antonio which, described in legal terms, is grotesque in its complexity: the scene opens with Shylock as plaintiff pursuing an action for breach of contract; it ends with Antonio (or more properly the state of Venice) as 'plaintiff' in a case in which Shylock defends himself against a charge of criminal conspiracy against a Venetian citizen. The impossible change of plea, the exchange of plaintiff and defendant, the intervention of Portia, these all confound strict principles. It is furthermore not wholly clear whether Portia's 'mercy' in this passage translates *clementia* or *misericordia*. If her plea is properly for mercy, then it is presumably a 'plea in mitigation', correctly made only after sentence has been passed; on the other hand, if she is pleading for clemency, this is to place the whole action of the scene outside normal Common Law procedure, transferring it to the realm of equity. In appealing to the quality of mercy, she is in fact appealing also beyond the strict operation of positive law to those qualities of which it can take no cognizance: the god-like compassion in the heart of kings which is given merely crude and inadequate expression in our fumbling attempts at legal equity. If therefore we find Shakespeare, demonstrably familiar with the terminology, the quirks and procedures of the law, and himself litigious in a highly litigious age, setting aside the rational and familiar processes of a court, he manifestly does so with dramatic purpose.

For the very violence done to legal process and terminology is itself conducted expertly. Before Shylock's delayed entry we are shown a court, which is about to stand upon the strictest niceties of legalistic interpretation, demonstrate its bias before the opening of the trial. The judge himself addresses the defendant with commiseration, and the plaintiff, when eventually he is summoned before the court, in terms of reprehension for his 'strange suit'. As the scene proceeds, forms of law are violated with a consistency and irony which argues expert knowledge on the dramatist's part and the audience's knowledgeable participation. For, on at least three occasions in the trial, elementary and generally accepted principles of law were set aside. The first concerns the substance of the trial itself, Antonio's 'forfeiture' or failure to meet his bond within the stipulated time. It had become universally the practice even by Shakespeare's day (and was given statutory recognition in Queen Anne's reign) that an appeal in equity against an intolerable forfeiture was set aside and an equitable 'penalty' (in this case the return of the principal with a just calculation of interest) substituted for the forfeit. In the second place, Shylock refuses a 'tender in open court' when Portia asks if Antonio is now able to repay the principal sum (IV.1.205–7):

PORTIA
Is he not able to discharge the money?
BASSANIO
Yes, here I tender it for him in the court,
Yea, twice the sum.

This offer would in fact have released Antonio from the penalties. But, in the third place, if we accept Portia's insistence that the 'tender' be set aside if Shylock will not avail himself of it, her quibble on the spilling of blood denies another legal maxim that any right assumes the conditions which make the exercise of the right possible; in this instance the right to take a pound of flesh presupposes the necessary condition of blood-shedding (we saw above that in *Zelauto* Cornelia succeeds, like Portia, with the same non-legal quibble).

These ambiguities and creative errors are the marks of a most delicate craftsmanship and imply a mature and judicious relationship between the dramatist and his audience, a substantial number of whom would be sophisticated men and members of the Inns of Court. The result is complex in that it unites contrary and even conflicting attitudes. There is no easy moral decision, no comfortable discrimination for the audience between gentle Christian and rapacious Jew; on the contrary it can be justly argued that the trial is 'rigged' and our sympathies therefore enlisted by simple reaction on behalf of Shylock – who has earlier put up a dignified and wholly acceptable plea for his essential humanity: 'Hath not a Jew eyes? Hath not a Jew hands, organs, dimensions, senses, affections, passions?'

But the contrary response is also valid. Neither Jew nor Christian in this play lives up to his formal or assumed profession of faith, but neither profession is thereby in itself invalidated. It is a crude impercipience that fails to recognize the Jewish sacramentalism in Shylock's proud rejection of Bassanio in Act One: 'I will not eat with you, drink with you, nor pray with you.' Equally, though we may hear it with some unease in the trial scene, Portia's declaration of faith has a like absolute validity (IV.1.193–7):

> *And earthly power doth then show likest God's*
> *When mercy seasons justice. Therefore, Jew,*
> *Though justice be thy plea, consider this:*
> *That in the course of justice none of us*
> *Should see salvation.*

As Shylock's pride in relation to Bassanio focuses centuries of ritual and sacramental law in the humblest Jewish household, so Portia's shift in meaning between human and divine justice in this speech focuses one of Shakespeare's deepest convictions, expressed in Claudius's passionate contrition (*Hamlet*, III.3.46–7):

> *Whereto serves mercy*
> *But to confront the visage of offence?*

or Isabella's plea to Angelo in *Measure for Measure* (II.2.59–63):

> *No ceremony that to great ones longs,*
> *Not the king's crown nor the deputed sword,*
> *The marshal's truncheon nor the judge's robe,*
> *Become them with one half so good a grace*
> *As mercy does.*

This plea is given its full theological argument some ten lines later, in which the Incarnation, divine justice, mercy and redemption are all given their due relation in terms which extend Portia's words in *The Merchant of Venice*:

> *Why, all the souls that were were forfeit once;*
> *And He that might the vantage best have took*
> *Found out the remedy. How would you be*
> *If He, which is the top of judgement, should*
> *But judge you as you are? O, think on that,*
> *And mercy then will breathe within your lips*
> *Like man new made.*

Here then we have the substance of the scriptural argument implied in the Lord's Prayer, 'forgive us our trespasses, as we forgive' (see the note on IV.1.198) and the prophetic command of Micah which would appeal equally to Shylock: 'What then doth the Lord require of thee but to do justly, to love mercy, and to walk humbly with thy God?' These three qualities, of justice, mercy, and humility, are constant *Leitmotiven* throughout the play. As our compassion therefore is demanded by Shylock's plight, and a profound unease experienced through the behaviour of the Christians (not least by the jarring inanity of Gratiano's exclamations, 'A Daniel . . . ! Mark, Jew!'), our critical faculties remain alert to the further implications of the scene: the implacability of Shylock's hate and the consequent ironic truth carried by the pun 'Not on thy sole, but on thy soul, harsh Jew'; the fundamental verities of the commonplaces in Portia's speech on mercy, even if by today we find them somewhat blown upon by repetition; our conviction that, by whatever devious means and with whatever shifts and quibbles, the essential charity of Antonio's assistance to Bassanio cannot be allowed a tragic outcome through a 'merry bond'. Nor do these convictions preclude our coming to astringent conclusions concerning the levity of the Venetians, the unseemly covetousness which mars both Christian and Jew in the play, and the bitter confrontation of two essentially noble minds, Antonio and Shylock, both flawed and overthrown by their deep-seated racial and personal antipathies, concentrated within the sharp acrimony of the trial.

Two matters remain to be considered in the exploration of the play's legal aspects. It might seem equivocal to hold the balance so nicely poised between the legal rivals in this scene which hovers so precariously on the brink of tragedy. But this equivocation, the placing of dramatic interest in the delicate discrimination of casuistic argument, was an accustomed and highly regarded exercise in rhetoric for the Elizabethans, and it would have been surprising if drama had not availed itself of this mode and benefited from it. Every grammar-school boy, every lawyer and preacher, was used to posing the 'rhetorical question' and weighing the argument with discrimination, as in Shake-speare's

> *To be or not to be – that is the question;*
> *Whether . . .*
> *Or . . .*
> *Thus . . .*
> *And thus . . .*

or Marlowe's

> *What is beauty, saith my sufferings then?*

which proceeds to an answer in the precise, argumentative form of an unrhymed sonnet. If the trial scene be thought of in such extended rhetorical terms, we shall not be far removed from the springs of its dramatic power. Shylock's claim, 'I stand for law', assumes many questions: What is equity between men? What form may mercy take, if it is not to destroy the necessary rigours of justice? With what right may imperfect men, by their office, pass judgement on others little or no worse than they? Lear invites us (IV.6.152–4) to 'See how yond justice rails upon yond simple thief . . . change places and, handy-dandy, which is the justice, which is the thief?' Arguing in the contrary sense, and pleading for the necessity of human judgement, Angelo in *Measure for Measure* (II.1.19–21) concedes that

> *The jury passing on the prisoner's life*
> *May in the sworn twelve have a thief or two*
> *Guiltier than him they try. . . .*

But this undoubted threat to all human justice does not absolve us from attempting the process. Indeed, the conclusion of this argument, embedded within the trial scene, is ultimately Portia's conviction that if man were to receive impartial justice and no more, in the perfect clarity of divine judgement 'none of us should see salvation'. In face of this fact (theological rather than legal in its intuition), human justice must do the best it can with its imperfect instruments.

We are fortunate that we have an exact parallel to this dramatic 'debate' in one of the probable sources of Shakespeare's play, Alexandre Silvayn's *The Orator*, published in its English translation in 1596. This is a volume of 'Declamations' or rhetorical debates in moral theology, in which many of the cases explored handle the teasing casuistry behind apparently straightforward cases in law.

Declamation 95 deals directly with the substance of Shylock's plot: 'Of a Jew, who would for his debt have a pound of the flesh of a Christian.' Of far more interest than the almost certain borrowings in detail from this work are the quality and substance of its argument, so close to the temper and implications of Shakespeare's trial scene. For it proceeds by formal disputation, the Jew putting his case, to which we have 'The Christian's Answer'. Its manner may be judged by brief quotations. The Jew claims that it is impossible

> *to break the credit of traffic amongst men without great detriment to the Commonwealth: wherefore no man ought to bind himself unto such covenants which he cannot or will not accomplish.*

The Christian answers:

> *It is no strange matter to hear those dispute of equity which are themselves most unjust; and such as have no faith at all, desirous that others should observe the same inviolable.* . . . *If then, when* [the Jews] *had newly received their law from God* . . . *they were so wicked, what may one hope of them now, when they have neither faith nor law, but their rapine and usuries?* . . . *It may please you then, most righteous Judge, to consider all these circumstances, having pity of him who doth wholly submit himself unto your just clemency.*

Shakespeare's fourth Act is no such 'Declamation', but, in the nice adjustment of its dramatic tones and human relationships, it preserves the same quality of disputation, weighing good against good, evil against evil.

In the second place, and in the same nicely adjusted temper, we are left in some ambiguity concerning the fate of Shylock as the scene concludes. Setting aside for the moment our unease at the duress under which Shylock assents to becoming a Christian, we find ourselves in some confusion arising from the technical terminology with which the Duke's judgement is pronounced. Its temper and intention are clear; Shylock has embarked on the trial carrying a knife and pair of balances, parody of the emblematic sword and scales of justice; at line 365 the process is complete and the Duke is about to pass judgement:

> That thou shalt see the difference of our spirit,
> I pardon thee thy life before thou ask it.

These words have perhaps a sourly self-righteous flavour after the bitter manoeuvres of the scene, but they represent no less than fact. And they introduce an unexpected conclusion, that in the event, contrary to expectation, Shylock suffers no material loss but a fine. The words demand close attention. The Duke first declares the appropriate penalty:

> For half thy wealth, it is Antonio's,
> The other half comes to the general state,
> Which humbleness may drive unto a fine.

Shylock, perhaps doubtful either of his own humility or the state's willingness to reduce the forfeit of the remaining half of his goods to a fine, assumes that he is faced with penury:

> Yóu take my life
> When you do take the means whereby I live.

Portia asks of Antonio the significant question, 'What mercy can you render him . . .?' (at this point *misericordia*), in mitigation of the sentence now passed. Antonio proposes a different disposition for each half of the penalty. The court is first asked 'To quit the fine for one half of his goods'. 'To quit for' is a curious grammatical use (see note to IV.1.378); if 'quit' retains its meaning of 'settling' or

30

'quittance' (in Hamlet's sense a 'quietus' or final settlement), it would seem that Shylock has even the fine remitted. For the second half of Shylock's goods, which might have been awarded Antonio as the aggrieved party, Antonio renounces any claim he might have to possess it himself but asks for it 'in use', a legal provision to secure the inheritance for Jessica and Lorenzo (see note to IV.1.380, where the legal details are specified). These provisions in turn reflect upon the demand that Shylock become a Christian, for Coryat, whose *Crudities* were published in 1611 after his tour in Italy and stay in Venice, describes the sardonic treatment of the baptized Jews: 'all their goods are confiscated as soon as they embrace Christianity' in order that this renunciation of their wealth may 'disclog their souls and consciences'. From this material humiliation Shylock is released.

There remain the spiritual penalties and in their several degrees we find them repugnant. Antonio's legal 'conveyance to user' of half the estate, securing Jessica's inheritance, is in fact a recognition forced upon Shylock of her conversion to Christianity and her marriage to a despised Gentile, a spendthrift and man of levity. Only if we give full emotional value to Shylock's terrible prayer (III.1. 81–2) that his apostate daughter may be hearsed at his feet, dead to him and to Jewry by her desertion of her faith, can we feel the impact of this humiliation, that Lorenzo the Christian shall inherit as his son-in-law. But what of his own conversion, to which he responds 'I am content'? We may argue formally that the sacrament of baptism will operate objectively, conveying grace to which Shylock has the opportunity of responding; certainly the 'conversion of the Jews' – a far-distant and unlikely event to Marvell in addressing his Coy Mistress – was something greatly to be desired. But this is precisely the point at which we feel most forcibly the 'tragedy' of the play. Until this point the conflict between Antonio and Shylock has proceeded dramatically at many levels simultaneously. Both are depicted as men grave to the point of austerity, and Shylock defines their antipathy with precision, the intersection of race, religion, and commercial morality at their most sensitive (I.3.39–42):

> *I hate him for he is a Christian;*
> *But more, for that in low simplicity*
> *He lends out money gratis and brings down*
> *The rate of usance here with us in Venice.*

At the conclusion of the trial scene the 'props' that sustain his life are removed more effectually than if he had been broken financially. He has failed to trap Antonio to his greatly desired death, he has been affronted at every point in his racial and religious pride, and he makes his exit broken as much by the apparent magnanimity of the court as by any physical adversity. His exit is one of the most puzzling moments on the Shakespearian stage. It is prob-able – if such a speculation may be allowed – that if this large theme had been handled by Shakespeare ten years later, the dramatic lines might well have been etched with greater firmness.

*

> *Ah, good old Mantuan! I may speak of thee as the traveller*
> *doth of Venice:*
> > Venetia, Venetia,
> > Chi non ti vede, non ti pretia.
> > > *Love's Labour's Lost,* IV.2.90–93

In physical setting the theatre has its own shorthand symbols for the Venetian scene; however bare the décor.

we are used to seeing the occasional gondola mooring-post, the outline of the Rialto bridge, or some surface detail from the Ca' d'Oro or a Palladian villa in the Brenta valley. But the setting and atmosphere of *The Merchant of Venice* pose problems beyond the superficial symbols. To the Elizabethan, Venice was probably the most evocative name in Europe. Its splendour – in decline, to be sure, but nonetheless splendour – was a commonplace, an atmosphere created for them from a hundred sources.

If they were travelling scholars consulting classical texts, their richest access to the Greeks was by way of the Venetian printing-house and particularly the press of Aldus Manutius; if they wanted philosophy, history, drama, the Aldine volumes provided, between about 1490 and 1510, the first printed editions of Plato and Aristotle, Thucydides and Herodotus, Sophocles and Aristophanes – though the chances were that if Shylock wished to read a printed version of Deuteronomy or Leviticus, he could obtain it more readily from the Gentile printing-house of Daniel Bomberg than from the more famous press of his fellow-Jew, Soncino; for Bomberg had been granted a complete monopoly of Hebrew printing in Venice for almost the whole of the first half of the sixteenth century. Italy had indeed learned the lessons of the German printers well and by 1500 there were some hundred and fifty presses in Venice alone. Dante and Boccaccio were handsomely available and Petrarch exerted complete dominance over the love sonnet throughout the century. If the scholar's mind moved to the epic, Ariosto was to his hand, and melancholy Torquato Tasso. If the traveller wished to bring back illustrated books Cesare Vecellio's *Habiti antichi et moderni* (1590) gave him detailed costumes, while Franco's *Habiti d'huomeni et donne venetiane* provided him with an engraving, 'Il Nouo Ponte de Rialto', only a few

years (1609) later than the meeting-place of Shylock and
Antonio.

Nor was the stay-at-home Londoner at a great disadvan-
tage. John Florio, a second-generation Italian exile, provided him, in *A World of Words* (1598), his earliest entry
to the Italian language; if he wished to acquire an italianate
precision in fencing, the master, Vincenzo Saviolo, was not
only a resident in London but provided the best manual to
the art, published in 1595. Italianate manners were more
ambiguous; if like Hamlet he would be 'the glass of
fashion', Baldassare Castiglione's *Il Libro del Cortegiano*
was 'done into English' in 1561 by Sir Thomas Hoby as
The Courtier, 'very necessary and profitable for young
gentlemen and gentlewomen abiding in court, palace, or
place', or Giovanni della Casa's *Galateo* (translated in
1576) gave them detailed directions of a more assimilable
and homely quality. The courtly ideal of the soldier-
scholar in Nerissa's commendation of Bassanio echoes the
fuller summary of these perfections in Ophelia's description of Hamlet: 'the courtier's, soldier's, scholar's, eye,
tongue, sword', a combination of qualities found historically at their highest in the family of Bassanio's former
patron, the Marquis of Montferrat (see note, I.2.108). This
soldierly courtliness had its other side in the swaggering
braggart which Portia is to imitate (III.4.60); the costume
of these 'bragging Jacks' was also to be seen in Vecellio's
Habiti as the 'Bravo Venetiano'.

London would also give him an adequate introduction to
Italian music, if only in the works of the remarkable
Ferrabosco family. The first Alfonso wrote in 1564 of his
'youth and health spent in the Queen's service' as Court
Musician. He was the friend of Morley and Byrd and in
1587 published in Venice two sets of five-part madrigals.
His son Alfonso was born at Greenwich, became Ben

Jonson's friend and composed the music for some of his masques, including *The Masque of Blackness* (1604), *The Masque of Beauty* (1607), and *The Masque of Queens* (1608). This collaboration established yet another artistic link with Venice by way of the theatre, for Jonson's other collaborator was Inigo Jones, the architect of Whitehall; in his architecture' and in the smaller scale of décor for the masques, Inigo Jones introduced Andrea Palladio (1518–80) to England, evolving the English version of that Palladianism which is still to be seen in its perfection in the villas of the Veneto, designed by Palladio. This (as we shall conjecture) was the atmosphere of Belmont, the quiet grace of the villa, retired from the commercial centre on the lagoon.

Shakespeare then had ample access to matters Venetian without necessarily stirring from London. He was made aware of Italian monetary power in those Lombardy merchant-bankers and men of wealth (who gave its name to Lombard Street). Some of these were intimates of the Court and it is not impossible that the influential Filippo Corsini, who lived in Gracechurch Street, arranged, in the closing year of Elizabeth's reign, the visit to London of Don Virginio Orsino who (if Leslie Hotson's conjectures are correct – and they are very beguiling) was present at the 'first night' of *Twelfth Night*.

But we can get still nearer two significant moments in *The Merchant of Venice*. At III.4.47–54, Portia instructs Balthasar in his part in her preparation for the defence of Antonio:

> *Take this same letter,*
> *And use thou all th'endeavour of a man*
> *In speed to Padua. See thou render this*
> *Into my cousin's hands, Doctor Bellario,*
> *And look what notes and garments he doth give thee*

> Bring them, I pray thee, with imagined speed
> Unto the traject, to the common ferry
> Which trades to Venice.

The common ferries, the *traghetti*, Shakespeare could have known from travellers' talk. The relations between Padua and Venice were more significant, a part of that pattern of scholarship which by the sixteenth century became an interchange of humanist learning across the Alps. The University of Padua had been under the protection and patronage of the Venetian Republic for a century when Colet studied there before returning to found St Paul's School and to write the most influential classical grammar of the sixteenth century. Almost exactly a century later William Harvey went to Padua to hear the mathematics lectures of Galileo, the precise contemporary of Shakespeare and Marlowe. Above all, Padua was Europe's finest faculty of law, worthy setting for the learned Bellario who should unravel, with Portia as his instrument, the strange judicial processes of the trial scene.

More organically related to the theme of the play was Shakespeare's palpable debt to the Academies which were established in sixteenth-century Italy. Avowedly based on Plato's Academia, a school of philosophical and practical training, the Italian Academies became the powerful centres of neo-platonic doctrine in Europe. At the Florentine Academy, founded by Vasari in 1562, artists and philosophers met to discuss matters of common interest, in particular those central doctrines of neo-platonism, the relation of matter to spirit, of body to soul, and of the hierarchy of the arts among themselves as revelations of divine truths. Shakespeare many times explored these doctrines in his plays. The opening of *Love's Labour's Lost* – and the subsequent development of the plot – makes witty play on the whole subject of Academies and academic learning; the King of Navarre, seeking to circumvent 'cormorant devouring Time' and rather to make his courtiers 'heirs of all eternity', becomes another Vasari:

> *Our late edict shall strongly stand in force:*
> *Navarre shall be the wonder of the world;*
> *Our court shall be a little Academe,*
> *Still and contemplative in living art.*

In *Timon of Athens* Shakespeare's debt was more particular, the Poet and Painter in the first scene echoing, in their argument over precedence, one of the most vigorous of the academic arguments, in which Leonardo da Vinci was himself involved, namely the disputed primacy of the verbal over the visual arts. But *The Merchant of Venice* contains the clearest and most extended of these echoes and in a form which would have commended it clearly to the members of any Italian Academy. In Belmont Lorenzo and Jessica await the outcome of Portia's feigned pilgrimage. The equivocal light of the moon leads them to a flyting-match of lovers, but this is subdued to a moving account of harmony and of heavenly motion (V.1.58–62):

> *Look how the floor of heaven*
> *Is thick inlaid with patens of bright gold.*
> *There's not the smallest orb which thou beholdest*
> *But in his motion like an angel sings,*
> *Still quiring to the young-eyed cherubins. . . .*

From the sacramental reference in 'paten' (or Communion dish) to the heavenly choir, this passage prepares for the statement of the neo-platonic commonplace which follows:

> *Such harmony is in immortal souls,*
> *But whilst this muddy vesture of decay*
> *Doth grossly close it in, we cannot hear it.*

The painters and philosophers of the Academies had evolved a mythology to express this contrast between the immortal soul and its 'muddy vesture' (its images are examined in Edgar Wind's *Pagan Mysteries in the Renaissance*), and in one of its forms this mythology involved the destruction of the body to release the soul, whether in its pagan form of Apollo's flaying of Marsyas or the martyrdom of St Bartholomew also by flaying (see the notes to V.1.64). As we shall see, this passage plays an important part in the closing structure of the play. Meanwhile we see it as yet another moment in that fruitful participation of English and European scholars and artists in that movement which we fitly know as the rebirth of classical antiquity.

Venice, then, hub of Italian commerce and one of the most potent centres of the arts, was a dramatic setting to which Shakespeare and his fellow dramatists were frequently to return, its glories and its corrupt decadence establishing tensions of which *The Merchant of Venice* and *Othello* were to make dramatic use. In this matter of physical setting, the very richness of the associations proves almost an embarrassment. Whether we confine ourselves to the simple evocative symbols of the Elizabethan theatre or the full-scale décor of the nineteenth-century stage, Venice is a relatively simple problem; artists from the great Mannerists, through Canaletto, Guardi, Turner, Ruskin, and Piper, have concentrated our picture of opulence and 'pleasing decay'. Belmont, however, is another matter and there remains a teasing ambiguity in its location and atmosphere throughout the play. It would not be alien to Shakespeare's way with proper names to make a contrast between the city of the lagoons, precariously and unhealthily wrested from the marshy delta, and 'Belmont', the fair upland retreat. This lies within the temper

of the play and there is a certain radiance in the movement
from Venice to Belmont which the theatre has generally
seized upon. But it is no simple contrast. The first two
scenes of the play open significantly with the same mood:
in Venice Antonio's malaise,

> *In sooth I know not why I am so sad.*
> *It wearies me, you say it wearies you . . .*

is echoed by Portia's in Belmont:

> *By my troth, Nerissa, my little body is aweary of this great*
> *world . . .*

and however it may be transformed into 'the rent that's
due to love', there is an uncomfortably frequent intrusion
of the commerce of Venice and its temper into the serenity
of Belmont. Nor does Shakespeare, in the Illyrian im-
precision of his topography, take any pains to elaborate his
Bel-mont. Such slight indications of place as we find appear
on occasion to give a hint of sea-coast, echoing the landing
of Jason at his goal (I.1.168–71):

> *For the four winds blow in from every coast*
> *Renownèd suitors, and her sunny locks*
> *Hang on her temples like a golden fleece,*
> *Which makes her seat of Belmont Colchos' strond. . . .*

But this is of course no more than metaphor and for the
most part the temper is that of the Palladian villas of the
Veneto, a retreat from the business of Venice.

The past quarter-century has seen the most vigorous
arguments concerning this whole matter of stage setting
for Shakespeare. On one side we have those who declare
a Shakespeare play to be a 'dramatic poem', with all the
décor 'in the words'. As a minimal setting for its presenta-
tion there has evolved a conception of an Elizabethan

theatre which was no more than a platform for declamation and though modern scholarship has disposed of this mythical theatre, too many critical assumptions still rest upon it. (For a sensible summary of current knowledge see R. A. Foakes, 'The Profession of Playwright' in Stratford-upon-Avon Studies 3, *Early Shakespeare*, 1961.) At the other end of the scale were the excesses of the nineteenth-century theatre from which so much of our present thinking and practice is a reaction. From Charles Kean to Beerbohm Tree, realism and visual elaborations were pursued for their own sakes to the great detriment of the play. A sensible and critically discriminating theatre practice adopts neither position. We should find it difficult now to deny the past three centuries of theatre history, nor did Shakespeare himself work in a visually impoverished theatre. In stage colour, symbolism, grouping, the theatrical context and machinery for the words was evocative, suggestive, reinforcing the spirit and argument of the words. The best contemporary décor does the same, and *The Merchant of Venice* provides an interesting case. Gordon Craig made some of his most important critical judgements on décor based on the drawings by his father, E. W. Godwin, which were published in *The Architect* in 1875. Commenting on them in a series of articles in *The Mask* in 1909–11, he said:

> *Either the producer was to represent that purely imaginative realm of the poetic drama removed from all realities, furnished and peopled with purely imaginative forms, or to give a reflection of reality as clear as the reflection of Narcissus in the pool.*

This was the temper of Godwin's essay on *The Merchant of Venice* which was furnished with the architect's drawings:

*The Venice of Shakespeare ... was then in the full swing
of the pride of life, and the very notion of decay or dilapida-
tion must have been hateful to her, all the more hateful from
an occasional gleam of consciousness that her power was
already rapidly decaying.*

Godwin therefore prescribes certain precise buildings as
his models for the décor, uniting grandeur and decay in the
temper with which he conceives Shakespeare to have
written. Gordon Craig's comment is just and has a more
universal application than our immediate concern:

*His work was the natural realistic link between the un-
imaginative and the imaginative. In the immediate tomorrow comes the next link in which the accessories shall
be not correct in data but correct in spirit; when we shall
not realize but suggest.*

This ideal of Gordon Craig has by no means been wholly
achieved. We have had realistic if not lavish Venices,
urbane, eighteenth-century Venices after Guardi, even
realizations of Mannerist sets, a dilution of Tintoretto.
More recently the precise rendering of place has been
given up almost entirely and – as in productions of *The
Merchant of Venice* during the 1960s at Stratford-upon-
Avon, and the production of *The Jew of Malta* (1963-5)
which was consciously a companion-piece – Malta, Venice,
and Belmont have been evoked more by the suggestion of
architectural texture, light, and mood than by any con-
crete reference to a building or element of topography. In
this respect we have seriously returned to the temper of
the Elizabethan theatre while not denying the physical de-
velopments (in lighting and machinery) in the theatre since
Shakespeare's day nor the shift in our visual consciousness
in the course of three centuries of European painting.

The 'problem of décor' then in *The Merchant of Venice*,

whether viewed historically or from the point of view of
the contemporary theatre, is relatively clear. Venice, it
seems fair to say, was an evocative name for Shakespeare,
representing all that was both creative and decadent in the
Italy of his day. It is obvious that he was writing with no
sharply defined sense of locality but with a complex feeling
for mood and 'cultural' significance. Giordano Bruno and
the new Philosophy, the disputes of the Academies, the
old economy and the new usury, the movement of race
and the fruitful relation of city and countryside, all these
were matters which found their place in the tensions and
complexities of the play; the text demands no more than a
setting in which these complexities are given a full and, if
possible, evocative context.

For the writing is as varied in its density and texture as
any play by Shakespeare until the period of his great
tragedies; if 'décor' and music in Shakespeare's day were
efficient and richly evocative of the mood of the play, they
had in *The Merchant of Venice* a play of great verbal complexity to serve. We have seen that in the theatre one of the
main problems for the director and the artist who provides
his visual setting is the delicate relationship between Venice
and Belmont, between the world of 'reality' amply interpreted down the ages by artists of distinction and that of
'fantasy', a Belmont whose secret is in fact as tough a hold
on reality as that of Venice. These transitions and overtones are very firmly established by the language of the
play, which fluctuates swiftly between the rhetoric of a
quite self-conscious sententiousness ('Good *sentences*, and
well pronounced' – I.2.10), through a flexible and witty
prose to a poetry whose biblical and classical rhythms
acknowledge an unusual indebtedness to some of Shakespeare's most frequently explored sources, such as Ovid,
Virgil, and the Bible.

There are three main worlds here to which the language gives entry. First, we have wealthy, febrile Venice, a city of rich appearance, of commerce and of masques, the tone of which is exactly caught by the evasive, high-sounding verse of Bassanio (I.1.122–5):

> 'Tis not unknown to you, Antonio,
> How much I have disabled mine estate
> By something showing a more swelling port
> Than my faint means would grant continuance.

This is a somewhat portentous description of a spendthrift, which, extended to an equally elaborate plea for aid, earns Antonio's proper – though still oblique – rebuke:

> You know me well, and herein spend but time
> To wind about my love with circumstance. . . .

Shylock's world is a cosmos within a cosmos, expressed in the greatest verbal variety, of grotesque prose, high rhetoric and measured scriptural tones. It is seen in its greatest flexibility when he speaks with his own kin and blood, with Tubal and with Jessica. With the former, the sharply grotesque can quickly attract to itself near-tragic tones (III.1.110–13):

> It was my turquoise; I had it of Leah when I was a bachelor. I would not have given it for a wilderness of monkeys.

And this can answer to a puritan gravity in his speech with Jessica which establishes the essentially alien temper of his Jewish world within the gaiety of Venice (II.5.27–36):

> What, are there masques? . . .
> Clamber not you up to the casements then,
> Nor thrust your head into the public street
> To gaze on Christian fools with varnished faces;

> *But stop my house's ears, I mean my casements;*
> *Let not the sound of shallow foppery enter*
> *My sober house. By Jacob's staff I swear*
> *I have no mind of feasting forth tonight . . .*

The tones of Belmont, the third and distinct world of the play, are clearly defined but of still greater variety, from the prose of Portia's exchanges with Nerissa ('God made him and therefore let him pass for a man') to the measured gravity of her submission both to her father's will and her new lord:

> *You see me, Lord Bassanio, where I stand,*
> *Such as I am . . .*

in which the formal word-play –

> *ambitious in my wish*
> *To wish myself much better . . . the full sum of me*
> *Is sum of something . . .*

– moves into the quiet and grave allegiance of a loving subject:

> *Happiest of all is that her gentle spirit*
> *Commits itself to yours to be directed,*
> *As from her lord, her governor, her king.*

When Shakespeare, then, came to write *The Merchant of Venice* he had at his command a range of dramatic verse and prose to express every modulation which the play's pattern demanded. In the transitions from the trial scene of the fourth Act to the closing tones of Belmont this range was tested to its furthest point in Shakespeare's early maturity.

●

'Mr Pope, when Macklin dies, you must write his epitaph.'
'That I will, madam,' said Pope, 'nay, I will give it now:
             Here lies the Jew
             That Shakespeare drew.'
                                    Kirkman, *Memoirs of Macklin* (1799)

*It is the duty of an actor always to know the passion and the
humour of each character so correctly, so intimately, and (if you
will allow the expression) to feel it so enthusiastically, as to be able
to define and describe it as a philosopher. . . . It is because Shakespeare knew the passions, their objects, and their operations, that
he has drawn them so faithfully.*
          Charles Macklin, 'The Art and Duty of an Actor' in
          Cooke, *Memoirs of Charles Macklin, Comedian* (1804)

It is not always easy to reconcile the functions – or the
conclusions – of the two great 'schools' of drama critics:
the scholar concerned with the 'dramatic poem', the 'extended metaphor', and that more potent if not always more
subtle critic, the actor. Hazlitt, who cannot be accused of
neglecting the theatre or underrating the actor's role, paid
oblique tribute to the power of a performance either to
establish or to warp the author's intention when he com-
plained of the stage that it 'is too often filled with traditional commonplace conceptions of the part, handed down
from sire to son, and suited to the taste of the great vulgar
and the small'. This was an aside when he was occupied
with a description of Edmund Kean's Shylock and it is a
notable quality of this play that the figure whom most
would consider to be the central character has been acted
with more irreconcilable lines of interpretation than any
other in Shakespeare. In 1701 Lord Lansdowne published
his adaptation under the title *The Jew of Venice*; this must
have received notable performance, with Betterton as
Bassanio and Mrs Bracegirdle as Portia. Shylock, however,
was played by Thomas Doggett and we may gather the

direction of his interpretation from the description of the gossipy Downes:

> *Mr Doggett, on the stage . . . is the only comic original now extant. Witness, Ben, Solon, Nikin, The Jew of Venice, etc.*

As early as 1709 Nicholas Rowe in the preface to his collected edition of Shakespeare protested against this line of interpretation:

> *We have seen the play received and acted as a comedy, and the part of the Jew perform'd by an excellent comedian, yet I cannot but think that it was designed tragically by the author.*

And the way was open for Macklin's innovation. We have many descriptions of his performances and they all demonstrate the remarkable range of his passion: 'sententious gloominess', 'sullen solemnity of deportment', 'a forcible and terrifying ferocity', these were the observations of a critic in the *Dramatic Censor* in 1770; Count Lichtenberg in 1775 extends it a little: 'He is slow, calm in his impenetrable cunning, and when he has the law on his side he is unflinching, even to the extreme of malice.' But the surviving portraits enhance the difficulty of interpretation. The popular engravings show Macklin in the trial scene, sardonic, dismissive and dominating the scene; the best-known caricature, in profile, shows an exaggerated nose and a pendulous lip. But Zoffany (1733/5–1810), the finest theatre artist of his day, paints a wholly different picture, a head, dishevelled and tragic, caught in the final plea after Portia's judgement. Whatever rough adaptations the eighteenth century tolerated, Shylock was no naïve villain.

The next major reinterpretation of the character was given one of its earliest performances at the Theatre Royal in Exeter on 3 December 1811 when Edmund Kean first performed Shylock in that city. Fifteen years earlier a 'Society of Gentlemen at Exeter' had been founded under a certain Dr Downman and one of their number, Richard Hole, the Vicar of Inwardleigh, wrote two essays, in 'Apology for the Character and Conduct' of Iago and of Shylock. The latter is undertaken with a pleasant wit ('let us reverse the case; and suppose that Shylock, a wealthy burgess of some jewish republic, had treated Antonio, an alien, a christian merchant, in the same manner') and the Deuteronomic regulations are used to good effect: 'at the time when the most enlightened nations of Europe were putting jews, infidels, and heretics to the sword, for the glory of God, the more tolerant disciples of Moses were content to pillage the purse, without taking the lives of those whom they conceived to be misbelievers'. It was conjectured by William Cotton, the historian of *The Drama in Exeter* (1887), that this Society of Gentlemen, patrons of the theatre, had influenced Kean in his portrayal of Shylock. Be that as it may, the performance in December 1811 certainly foreshadowed the success in Drury Lane in January 1814. Cotton writes:

> *Kean's Shylock was quite an original conception of the character; the popular idea was to pander to the prejudices of the public by making the Jew as hateful as possible. . . . He was represented in the guise of a dirty, objectionable old man, dressed in seedy habiliments, with a red Judas wig. Kean, despite the sarcasms of the conventional critics, adopted a respectable black wig, a clean countenance and a decent gown; he raised him to the dignity of a man and an ill-used man, and without attempting to condone the vices of his character, contrived to excite even pity for his misfortune.*

Kean's later success in London followed this line of interpretation, and Shylock has ever since oscillated between the malignant caricature and the dignified tragic 'hero'. E. W. Godwin, for all the scholarly sobriety of his designs for *The Merchant of Venice* in 1875 (p. 40 above), concedes the current Victorian assumption that at Shylock's exit the play is virtually over: 'The fifth Act, and indeed the whole episode of the rings, might very well be omitted in modern stage representation.' Henry Irving assumed, according to a contemporary account, 'that Shakespeare intended to enlist our sympathies on the side of the Jew'. 'The whole force of an "old, untainted religious aristocracy" is made manifest in his person.' (We are reminded that at the beginning of the nineteenth century Edmund Kean had seemed, in the words of Douglas Jerrold, 'like a chapter of Genesis'.) These are the phrases that traverse accounts of Irving's performances: 'an almost tragic elevation and grace'; 'pitiless, majestic, implacable'; and finally 'superb calm', even when the trial turns against him: 'the scales drop from his hands, but that is all'.

Here then are the broad lines and Edwin Booth summarizes them (though modifying some of the accepted views of the great traditional performances):

I believe that Burbage, Macklin, Cooke, and Kean ... made Shylock what is technically termed a 'character' part – grotesque in 'make up' and general treatment. . . . I think Macready was the first to lift the uncanny Jew out of the darkness of his native element of revengeful selfishness into the light of the venerable Hebrew, the Martyr, the Avenger.

Along these lines all performances of the play in this century have made their choice; the major critical interpretation latent in the actor's decision between the grotesque and the heroic has characterized such recent accounts of the part as those of Ralph Richardson (strongly in the tradition of Macklin and Kean), Michael Redgrave (as in every Shakespearian role by this actor, a considered, scholar's performance), and Peter O'Toole (a grave, prophetic figure in early middle age, yet capable of swift eruptions of feeling from the grotesque to the tragic).

Upon these decisions, which the play evidently allows the actor of integrity to make, much of our critical assumption concerning the nature of this play will depend. For this is Shylock's play in the theatre until the conclusion of the trial scene removes him from the action. Upon the stresses and nuances in portraying Shylock the main critical burden lies, whether in considering this play for the stage or ultimately in determining its central significance for the reader.

At the same time we recognize that Shakespeare set himself – and us – a formidable dramatic problem in establishing, if only in part, 'the villain as hero'. If Shylock does in fact 'steal the show', and remain most vividly in the collective theatrical memory from the past, Shakespeare has succeeded in conquering a fundamental dramatic prejudice; he has succeeded moreover in this, despite the fact that he removes this dominating figure for the concluding fifth of the work. We have then to see whether there is a counterpoise to this hazardous aim of creating a figure of heroic stature from one who is both socially and dramatically ambiguous. We find this balance, of course, in the character of Portia; indeed it may be said that if Shylock is to reach his full stature, Portia must also be played to the utmost range of her character; and conversely, if Portia is to be seen to the full extent of her complexity, Shylock has to realize in the fourth Act all the manifold potentialities of his character. A mere vice, a morality villain, would be no adversary, nor would the objective quality of grace and the law – despite the unworthiness of their Venetian ministers – be vindicated against a man of straw. Shylock and Portia are necessary foils to each other and beside them the other characters, even Bassanio and Antonio on whom so much turns, are men of diminished stature.

The determination of Portia's quality poses wholly different critical problems from those in which Shylock involves us. The perspective of Shylock's character, established by the tones of voice of the other characters, is uniform: he is either contemned or execrated; he is a dog or a devil. The complexity arises solely from the disparity between this universal condemnation and the dignified claims, enforcing on occasion a reluctant assent, which he makes on his own behalf. He is a man and a Jew, on each count a being of dignity, of grave and formidable power. Portia on the other hand is no simple creature either in her own or others' estimation. We meet her first in Bassanio's description and it is not easy to determine whether the order of his praise reflects upon her qualities or his own. She is 'richly left [... fair ... |Of wondrous virtues' (I.1. 161–3). In the next scene we meet her in her own person, speaking, after her first expression of *ennui*, in witty prose. She is in fact nicely poised between a proper subservience to her father's will and a caustic rejection of all the suitors brought to her court by his device, for there is both comic deprecation and humility in her final summary of her case (I.2.100–102):

> *If I live to be as old as Sibylla, I will die as chaste as Diana unless I be obtained by the manner of my father's will.*

Morocco leads us to a different perspective and he is uncomfortably articulate on her central attraction for the suitors. Bassanio had partly concealed his fundamental

seeking of wealth under the inflated image of the Golden
Fleece. Morocco is both more elaborate and more direct
(II.7.38–59):

> *All the world desires her;*
> *From the four corners of the earth they come*
> *To kiss this shrine, this mortal breathing saint.*
>   *... They have in England*
> *A coin that bears the figure of an angel*
> *Stampèd in gold – but that's insculped upon;*
> *But here an angel in a golden bed*
> *Lies all within.*

The progression is important: 'shrine – saint – angel [the
coin] – golden bed', a movement through images of rever-
ential worship, through wealth to marriage (for wealth).
Literary hindsight from a play, Ben Jonson's *Volpone*,
performed some ten years after *The Merchant of Venice*,
makes an uncomfortable comment on Morocco's imagery.
Volpone opens the play with Morocco's precise figure and
this time it is unambiguously directed to wealth:

> *Good morning to the day; and next my gold!*
> *Open the shrine that I may see my saint.*

Here the setting, 'the golden bed', is a shrine, a reliquary
or a monstrance, all of them terms of religious import, a
blasphemous transference of worship from the holy to the
material. Our discomfort in the scene of Morocco's choice
in *The Merchant of Venice* arises in part from our intuition
that his words alone make the correct equation of Portia
with wealth which is latent in the quest of all the suitors
and not least Bassanio.

Portia is also made an ambiguous figure by the many
classical parallels and allusions with which she and her
activities are surrounded. The first is a matter of historical

reference. Bassanio mitigates the unfortunate impression given by his initial description of the 'lady richly left' by continuing (I.1.165–6):

> *Her name is Portia, nothing undervalued*
> *To Cato's daughter, Brutus' Portia . . .*

Shakespeare was again to develop this character, for she was wife to Brutus who conspired with Cassius against Julius Caesar. She was the daughter of Cato Uticensis, a man of particular rectitude and himself one of Caesar's enemies. Portia in *The Merchant of Venice*, a woman of decisive action and concern for legal and social equity, is appropriately linked with the historical figure who, in *Julius Caesar*, can claim:

> *Think you I am no stronger than my sex,*
> *Being so fathered, and so husbanded?*

The parallels from mythology are more disquieting and turn upon two figures, Medea by association with the Golden Fleece, and, more explicitly, Hesione, who was rescued by Hercules.

It is clear that Shakespeare, in this play and elsewhere, was much preoccupied with Ovid's *Metamorphoses* and there are many direct allusions to Arthur Golding's influential translation which appeared in 1567. The seventh book seems to have been much in his mind (almost certainly indeed under his eye) as he wrote *The Merchant of Venice*. Here Ovid handles the disquieting climax of the Argonauts' quest for the Golden Fleece, the marriage of Jason and Medea and their departure from Colchis, and finally the almost necromantic rejuvenation of Jason's father, 'old Aeson'. Shakespeare's recollection of Golding's version begins early (I.1.169), with Bassanio's first description of Portia:

her sunny locks
Hang on her temples like a golden fleece,
Which makes her seat of Belmont Colchos' strond,
And many Jasons come in quest of her.

Many details establish a curious half-identification of
Portia with Medea, who, in Golding's translation, is made
part of Jason's triumphant capture of the fleece:

And so with conquest and a wife he loosed from
* Colchos strond*

(where the spelling is itself perhaps an indication of
Shakespeare's debt). Medea's father, the king of Colchis,
resembled Portia's father in setting a triple test of the
adventurers' wit, while there might well be uneasy undertones in Portia's concern lest she help Bassanio to choose
aright, if the Elizabethan audience recollected Medea's
assistance to Jason in circumventing her father's tests.
Indeed, we are kept ironically within the realm of myth in
the scene of Bassanio's choice as he, who had set out on
his quest in an avowed desire for gold, rejects the casket of
gold as 'Hard food for Midas'. Nor did the second half of
Ovid's seventh book escape Shakespeare, for the horrifying
description of Medea's enchantments as she addresses her
'charms and witchcrafts' to 'triple Hecat' in order to
renew 'Aeson's aged corse' is an incident most strangely
recalled by Jessica in the fifth Act.

*   In such a night*
Medea gathered the enchanted herbs
That did renew old Aeson.

This is in every way an odd conjunction of ideas, for, as
we have seen, it is not an isolated reference at the beginning and end of the play but is confirmed by the quite
deliberate identification by Gratiano (III.2.241): 'We are

the Jasons, we have won the Fleece.' The same uneasy
relation of the wooing of Portia with material reward is
made in her implied identification with Hesione who was
rescued by Hercules (see the note to III.2.55). As Bassanio
makes his choice, he is likened by Portia to Alcides (Hercules, whose feat of rescue is described in *Metamorphoses*,
XI):

> *Now he goes,*
> *With no less presence but with much more love*
> *Than young Alcides when he did redeem*
> *The virgin tribute paid by howling Troy*
> *To the sea monster.*

These parallels must not of course be pressed too far –
though Shakespeare does appear to elaborate them at
highly charged dramatic moments. It is noteworthy, at the
same time, that Portia expresses at least unconscious irony
in her 'much more love', contrasting the material motive
with which Hercules fights the sea monster with the implied single-mindedness of Bassanio's love.

Portia, indeed, is no simple heroine. In the first three
Acts the heiress of Belmont may be seen in an almost
wholly romantic light as a corrective to the darker tones of
Venice – *almost* wholly romantic, for even here, as we have
seen, there are both conscious and unconscious ironies in
the characterization and a curious echo of the material
cupidity of the Venetians. In the fourth Act she becomes
a dominant figure, witty, hard even to the point of risking
her quality of compassion, at certain moments a vehicle
for an abstract justice which her own associates violate.
For she has a strange role to sustain, poised between the
dignity, the inflexible racial and religious pride, and the
covetousness of Shylock on the one hand, and the levity,
the casual greed, and the fundamental grace of the Venetians

on the other. Shakespeare's success in fusing this strange mixture of attributes in Portia is tested by the fifth Act.

After Shylock's exit the dramatist is left with a concluding Act which must retain the dramatic power of the trial but in a wholly different key. To judge the raw material with which he worked we must return to Bassanio's choice of the casket in Act III, scene 2. The background has been carefully prepared. Bassanio, a 'prodigal', who, even in pleading for financial help from his friend Antonio, 'winds about with circumstance', is an ambiguous suitor for the lady 'of wondrous virtues'. The terms of his choice, the arguments concerning false appearance and the reality it conceals, are sententious and conventional enough. But the scene takes on a different intensity with Portia's acceptance of his suit (lines 149–50):

> *You see me, Lord Bassanio, where I stand,*
> *Such as I am . . .*

The graceful humility of the relationship, the masking of Bassanio's sudden elevation to riches by the conscious dignity accorded to his new status and authority – 'Lord Bassanio' – serve also to raise the fortune-hunter to a nobler quality; to borrow terms from another sphere, in being 'deemed' noble he has the opportunity of becoming so, a common experience in Shakespeare's mature comedies, one shared by Angelo, by the opalescent Orsino, by Bertram. This momentary exaltation of Bassanio is quickly subdued by grave news of Antonio, the transition characteristically marked by a punning play between Gratiano and Salerio (lines 239–42):

GRATIANO
> *How doth that royal merchant, good Antonio?*
> *I know he will be glad of our success;*
> *We are the Jasons, we have won the Fleece.*

SALERIO

I would you had won the fleece [fleets] *that he hath lost.*

In this darker mood the trial is prepared for and Shylock
dominates the succeeding movement.

This, then, is the dramatic temper that has to be
recreated and transfigured in the fifth Act. The ground is
again prepared by the business of the rings, wittily com-
plicated at every stage. The rings 'given and exchanged'
are gravely enough the 'matter of the sacrament of marriage' between the couples; Portia gives hers with as much
gravity as comedy permits (III.2.171–3):

> this ring,
> *Which when you part from, lose, or give away,*
> *Let it presage the ruin of your love ...*

– a gravity which in another context, like Othello's kerchief,
might become the matter of tragedy. After the trial the
same ring is pleaded as a reward for a friend's life and as
Bassanio yields it, returning it in fact to Portia, its original
owner, the central theme of the 'commerce of love' is
locked up: Antonio has jeopardized his life, Portia has
yielded her wealth in the token of this ring –

> *This house, these servants, and this same myself*
> *Are yours, my lord's. I give them with this ring*

– and the interchange is now complete (if as yet unrecog-
nized) at the end of the fourth Act, in ducats, persons,
wealth, and symbols.

The last Act opens strangely. Lorenzo and his 'infidel'
have been given an unearned dignity, in the stewardship
of Belmont during Portia's absence in Venice. Their witty
contest 'in such a night' plays on the Chaucerian and
Ovidian martyrs of love (see the notes to the opening
twenty-three lines of the fifth Act) but though these

'martyrs' have good literary antecedents, they sound strange in the teasing exchange of lovers' badinage. Cressid, Thisbe, Dido have all of them overtones beyond the merely tragic, involving also elements of duplicity, misconception, even treachery, which prepare for the introduction of Medea, surely a fateful name in this muster-roll of 'Good Women'. Not only does Medea at this point establish a strange, an alien gravity in the 'playful' opening to the Act which should bring the play to a radiant conclusion; Medea, particularly in the role of restorer of youth to 'old Aeson', ominously concludes the theme of Jason's quest which traverses the play. It is not for nothing that Arthur Golding's *Metamorphoses*, to which Shakespeare is throughout indebted, associates Medea with

> *Hecate, of whom the witches hold*
> *As of their goddess*

and that Jason

> *sware to take her to his wife*
> *By triple Hecate's holy rites.*

For Shakespeare's references to Hecate, in the tragic contexts of *Macbeth*, *Hamlet*, or *Lear*, or in the unlikely atmosphere of comedy (as Puck declares his final allegiance to this queen of darkness and governor of witchcraft at the conclusion of *A Midsummer Night's Dream*), have peculiarly ominous undertones – and, by implication, they intrude here again. It is with a suggestion of this dark tone that the lovers conclude their flyting-match with punning and none too happy references to Jessica's elopement, as she did 'steal from the wealthy Jew'.

With Stephano's entrance, announcing the return of Portia from her 'pilgrimage', Belmont's music, divine harmony, the soul's conquest over the body's 'muddy vesture', all seem to be the appropriate resolution of the play's disharmonies. But it would be a mistake to assume that Shakespeare accepts a facile neo-platonic conclusion of this kind – which too great concentration on Lorenzo's account of the function of music might lead us to assume. We are in fact still reminded, at the end of the play, of the wealth the search for which has led to so much covetous corruption throughout the play. Now, however, the very casualness with which Antonio is told of the safety of his argosies, the swift endowing of Lorenzo and Jessica with the anticipation of Shylock's wealth, the very relaxed ease of Belmont, all these establish the positive values of goods and wealth without laying too great stress upon them. The body too is much more than a 'muddy vesture', as the close of the play wittily insists; it is in fact an instrument of love, while love itself may borrow metaphors from the world of commerce, which has hitherto in the play been of so ambiguous standing.

The greatest of medieval Welsh poets, Dafydd ap Gwilym, has a phrase, 'cariad taladwy', which Gwyn Williams has extended in translation to 'the rent that's due to love'.* This 'rent' is acknowledged in *The Merchant of Venice* in many ways, by Antonio, by Jessica, by Portia, and by Bassanio, and it is exacted violently from Shylock on behalf of a daughter of doubtful desert. One rent remains to be paid in the happy fulfilment of all their

---

* Chaucer, in *The Book of the Duchess* (lines 764–8), gives the fullest expression of this aspect of courtly love:

> *Dredeles, I have ever yit*
> *Be tributarie and yiven rente*
> *To Love, hooly with good entente,*
> *And throgh plesaunce become his thral*
> *With good wille, body, herte, and al.*

This may be thoroughly conventional, but poets of the stature of Chaucer and Shakespeare have the habit of transfiguring convention.

marriages; it is acknowledged and promised in the punning extension of the word 'ring', in the happy bawdy of sensual love; and in neither reading nor performance may the closing lines be seen as mere levity. It is given to Antonio and Portia gravely to complete the formal interchange of tokens (lines 249-55):

ANTONIO

I once did lend my body for his wealth,
Which but for him that had your husband's ring
Had quite miscarried. I dare be bound again,
My soul upon the forfeit, that your lord
Will never more break faith advisedly.

PORTIA

Then you shall be his surety. Give him this,
And bid him keep it better than the other.

In his former bond for Bassanio's sake, Antonio had pledged no more than his flesh; now for both their sakes he is bound again, his 'soul upon the forfeit'. And in a final, almost casual gesture, the 'commerce of love' returns upon him in Portia's news of his argosies, 'richly come to harbour'.

Nor in this characteristic mixture of grave and gay should the reader forget that in an Elizabethan performance Portia's company of instrumentalists, her 'music', would have a final duty, of great importance in the dramatic stress and structure of the play. For the action would end not with words but, like all 'festive comedy' in a stately dance. For the end of these romantic comedies is marriage, and life, like a fairy-tale, 'happy ever after'. But the sacrament cannot with propriety be rendered on the stage; instead we have, in *As You Like It*, a formal masque of Hymen, in *Twelfth Night* the grave, precise words of the priest describing the marriage of Sebastian and Olivia, where the theology of the sacrament is exactly placed:

> *A contract of eternal bond of love,*
> *Confirmed by mutual joinder of your hands,*
> *Attested by the holy close of lips,*
> *Strengthened by interchangement of your rings;*
> *And all the ceremony of this compact*
> *Sealed in my function, by my testimony;*
> *Since when, my watch hath told me, toward my grave*
> *I have travelled but two hours.*

So here in *The Merchant of Venice* there would be the customary gracious dance, the couples united as they move from the stage, to the music with which the beauty of this Act has been initiated after the darkness of Act IV and its satiric aftermath in the witty conflict of Lorenzo and Jessica. T. S. Eliot quotes words in 'East Coker' which very precisely express this conclusion of true comedy:

> *The association of man and woman*
> *In daunsinge, signifying matrimonie –*
> *A dignified and commodious sacrament.*
> *Two and two, necessarye coniunction,*
> *Holding eche other by the hand or the arm*
> *Whiche betokeneth concorde.*

This 'concord' has been hard-won in *The Merchant of Venice* but it is achieved with a gracious dignity and with wit.

FURTHER READING

THE most convenient edition for study is John Russell Brown's new Arden edition (1955), which covers the textual problem and reprints many of the sources. The introduction to the New Cambridge edition by Arthur Quiller-Couch and J. Dover Wilson (1926) is well worth reading, and if more detail is needed, especially in theatre history up to its date of publication, the Furness Variorum edition (1888) should be consulted.

The most recent brief (but lively and dissident) study is A. D. Moody's *The Merchant of Venice* in the series Studies in English Literature (1964; general editor, David Daiches); it is the most serious work to be wholeheartedly critical of the Venetian Christians: 'the play does not celebrate a triumph of virtue over vice, but rather instructs the imagination in the deceptions and delusions that may attend upon goodly appearance and romantic prejudice'. An important essay taking the other viewpoint is Frank Kermode's 'The Mature Comedies' in *Early Shakespeare*, Stratford-upon-Avon Studies 3 (1961), which also contains J. R. Brown's 'The Realization of Shylock'. J. R. Brown's earlier book, *Shakespeare and His Comedies* (1957), should be read in particular for the concept of 'the usury of love'. G. Wilson Knight's *Shakespearian Production* (1964; first published in 1936 as *Principles of Shakespearian Production*) has two long sections devoted to this play from the point of view of the actor and producer. We are now glad to have the *Complete Pelican Shakespeare* edited by Alfred Harbage in a one-volume edition published in England in 1969; unhappily the introduction to *The Merchant of Venice* by Brents Stirling is rather perfunctory.

Among the more general studies which should be consulted for illuminating comments on this play are: C. L. Barber,

Shakespeare's Festive Comedy (1959), M. C. Bradbrook, *Shakespeare and Elizabethan Poetry* (1957; Peregrine Books 1964) and her *The Growth and Structure of Elizabethan Comedy* (1955; Peregrine Books 1963). Bertrand Evans, in *Shakespeare's Comedies* (1961), examines the plays from a very particular point of view, the awareness of the action by the protagonists.

The sources of the play are best examined in the first volume of Geoffrey Bullough's *Narrative and Dramatic Sources of Shakespeare* (1958); in the introduction to the Arden edition; in Kenneth Muir's *Shakespeare's Sources* (1957); and in *Elizabethan Love Stories*, edited by T. J. B. Spencer (Penguin Shakespeare Library 1968). It will be seen from the notes to this edition that, after the Bishops' Bible, the main Elizabethan work cited is Arthur Golding's translation of Ovid, *The XV Bookes of P. Ovidius Naso, entytuled Metamorphosis* (1567; latest reprint 1961).

The materials for studying the contemporary Italian scene are prolific. Two good general introductions are: J. R. Hale, *England and the Italian Renaissance* (1954), and A. Lytton Sells, *The Italian Influence in English Poetry* (1955). Mario Praz is always learned and stimulating and his early *Machiavelli and the Elizabethans* (1928) is still worth reading. It is even more important to read the Italian works in the Elizabethan translations and the English works influenced by Italy (e.g. Thomas Nashe, *The Unfortunate Traveller*, 1594; available in Thomas Nashe, *Selected Works*, edited by Stanley Wells in the Stratford-upon-Avon Library, 1964, and in Thomas Nashe, '*The Unfortunate Traveller*' *and Other Works*, edited by J. B. Steane, Penguin English Library, 1972). The most important of the Italian works are Castiglione's *The Courtier* (Sir Thomas Hoby's translation, Everyman's Library), Giovanni della Casa's *Galateo* (Penguin Classics, 1958), Tasso's *Jerusalem Delivered* (translated by Fairfax), and the sonnets of Petrarch (usefully studied in selection in the *Penguin Book of Italian Verse*, 1958).

For the economic background and usury in particular, R. H. Tawney is still the best guide, beginning with his *Religion and the Rise of Capitalism* (1926; Pelican Books 1938) and continuing in detail with his *Business and Politics and James I* (1958). There is also the valuable edition of Thomas Wilson's *Discourse upon Usury* (1572; edited by Tawney, 1925). The fullest literary application of these economic arguments is L. C. Knights, *Drama and Society in the Age of Jonson* (1937; Peregrine Books 1962).

This is the most tricky period in English law, involving the struggle between the Civil and the Common Lawyers, particularly after James's accession. The best scholarly treatment is the fourth volume of W. S. Holdsworth's *History of English Law* (1924, revised 1964–5); there are admirable things in Chapters 5, 6, 7, and 9 of F. W. Maitland's *Selected Historical Essays* (1957) and the available material from the Elizabethan period is surveyed in W. M. Merchant's 'Lawyer and Actor: Process of Law in Elizabethan Drama' in *English Studies Today*, 3 (1964).

We have now a clearer picture of the presence and activities of Jews in England before and during Shakespeare's day. Two books in particular are valuable: Cecil Roth, *A History of the Jews in England* (1941), and J. L. Cardozo, *The Contemporary Jew in Elizabethan Drama* (1925).

THE MERCHANT OF VENICE

THE CHARACTERS IN THE PLAY

THE DUKE OF VENICE
THE PRINCE OF MOROCCO⎱
THE PRINCE OF ARRAGON⎰ suitors of Portia
ANTONIO, a merchant of Venice
BASSANIO, his friend, suitor of Portia
PORTIA, the Lady of Belmont
SHYLOCK, a Jew of Venice
GRATIANO⎫
SALERIO ⎬ friends of Antonio and Bassanio
SOLANIO ⎭
LORENZO, in love with Jessica
NERISSA, Portia's waiting-woman
JESSICA, daughter of Shylock
TUBAL, a Jew of Venice, Shylock's friend
LEONARDO, servant of Bassanio
BALTHASAR⎱
STEPHANO ⎰ servants of Portia

LAUNCELOT GOBBO, servant of Shylock
OLD GOBBO, father of Launcelot

Magnificoes of Venice, Officers of the Court of Justice, a
Gaoler, Servants, and other Attendants

For Salarino, see page 163.

ANTONIO

In sooth I know not why I am so sad.
It wearies me, you say it wearies you;
But how I caught it, found it, or came by it,
What stuff 'tis made of, whereof it is born,
I am to learn;
And such a want-wit sadness makes of me
That I have much ado to know myself.

SALERIO

Your mind is tossing on the ocean,
There where your argosies with portly sail,
Like signors and rich burghers on the flood,   10
Or as it were the pageants of the sea,
Do overpeer the petty traffickers
That curtsy to them, do them reverence,
As they fly by them with their woven wings.

SOLANIO

Believe me, sir, had I such venture forth,
The better part of my affections would
Be with my hopes abroad. I should be still
Plucking the grass to know where sits the wind,
Peering in maps for ports and piers and roads,
And every object that might make me fear   20
Misfortune to my ventures, out of doubt
Would make me sad.

SALERIO   My wind cooling my broth
Would blow me to an ague when I thought
What harm a wind too great might do at sea.

I should not see the sandy hour-glass run
But I should think of shallows and of flats,
And see my wealthy Andrew docked in sand,
Vailing her high-top lower than her ribs
To kiss her burial. Should I go to church
And see the holy edifice of stone
And not bethink me straight of dangerous rocks,
Which touching but my gentle vessel's side
Would scatter all her spices on the stream,
Enrobe the roaring waters with my silks,
And in a word, but even now worth this,
And now worth nothing? Shall I have the thought
To think on this, and shall I lack the thought
That such a thing bechanced would make me sad?
But tell not me; I know Antonio
Is sad to think upon his merchandise.

ANTONIO

Believe me, no. I thank my fortune for it
My ventures are not in one bottom trusted,
Nor to one place; nor is my whole estate
Upon the fortune of this present year.
Therefore my merchandise makes me not sad.

SOLANIO

Why then you are in love.

ANTONIO   Fie, fie!

SOLANIO

Not in love neither? Then let us say you are sad
Because you are not merry; and 'twere as easy
For you to laugh and leap, and say you are merry
Because you are not sad. Now by two-headed Janus,
Nature hath framed strange fellows in her time:
Some that will evermore peep through their eyes
And laugh like parrots at a bagpiper,
And other of such vinegar aspect

That they'll not show their teeth in way of smile
Though Nestor swear the jest be laughable.

Enter Bassanio, Lorenzo, and Gratiano

Here comes Bassanio your most noble kinsman,
Gratiano, and Lorenzo. Fare ye well;
We leave you now with better company.

SALERIO

I would have stayed till I had made you merry,   60
If worthier friends had not prevented me.

ANTONIO

Your worth is very dear in my regard.
I take it your own business calls on you,
And you embrace th'occasion to depart.

SALERIO

Good morrow, my good lords.

BASSANIO

Good signors both, when shall we laugh? Say, when?
You grow exceeding strange. Must it be so?

SALERIO

We'll make our leisures to attend on yours.

Exeunt Salerio and Solanio

LORENZO

My Lord Bassanio, since you have found Antonio,
We two will leave you; but at dinner-time   70
I pray you have in mind where we must meet.

BASSANIO

I will not fail you.

GRATIANO

You look not well, Signor Antonio.
You have too much respect upon the world;
They lose it that do buy it with much care.
Believe me, you are marvellously changed.

ANTONIO

I hold the world but as the world, Gratiano,

71

A stage where every man must play a part,
And mine a sad one.

GRATIANO   Let me play the fool;
80 With mirth and laughter let old wrinkles come,
And let my liver rather heat with wine
Than my heart cool with mortifying groans.
Why should a man whose blood is warm within
Sit, like his grandsire cut in alabaster?
Sleep when he wakes? And creep into the jaundice
By being peevish? I tell thee what, Antonio,
I love thee, and 'tis my love that speaks:
There are a sort of men whose visages
Do cream and mantle like a standing pond,
90 And do a wilful stillness entertain
With purpose to be dressed in an opinion
Of wisdom, gravity, profound conceit,
As who should say, 'I am Sir Oracle,
And when I ope my lips, let no dog bark.'
O my Antonio, I do know of these
That therefore only are reputed wise
For saying nothing, when I am very sure
If they should speak, would almost damn those ears,
Which hearing them would call their brothers fools.
100 I'll tell thee more of this another time.
But fish not with this melancholy bait
For this fool gudgeon, this opinion.
Come, good Lorenzo. Fare ye well awhile;
I'll end my exhortation after dinner.

LORENZO
Well, we will leave you then till dinner-time.
I must be one of these same dumb wise men,
For Gratiano never lets me speak.

GRATIANO
Well, keep me company but two years more,
Thou shalt not know the sound of thine own tongue.

ANTONIO

   Fare you well; I'll grow a talker for this gear.   110

GRATIANO

   Thanks i'faith; for silence is only commendable
   In a neat's tongue dried and a maid not vendible.

                          Exeunt Gratiano and Lorenzo

ANTONIO Is that anything now?

BASSANIO Gratiano speaks an infinite deal of nothing,
   more than any man in all Venice. His reasons are as two
   grains of wheat hid in two bushels of chaff: you shall
   seek all day ere you find them, and when you have them
   they are not worth the search.

ANTONIO

   Well, tell me now what lady is the same
   To whom you swore a secret pilgrimage,   120
   That you today promised to tell me of.

BASSANIO

   'Tis not unknown to you, Antonio,
   How much I have disabled mine estate
   By something showing a more swelling port
   Than my faint means would grant continuance.
   Nor do I now make moan to be abridged
   From such a noble rate; but my chief care
   Is to come fairly off from the great debts
   Wherein my time, something too prodigal,
   Hath left me gaged. To you, Antonio,   130
   I owe the most in money and in love,
   And from your love I have a warranty
   To unburden all my plots and purposes
   How to get clear of all the debts I owe.

ANTONIO

   I pray you, good Bassanio, let me know it,
   And if it stand as you yourself still do,
   Within the eye of honour, be assured

My purse, my person, my extremest means
Lie all unlocked to your occasions.

BASSANIO

140 In my schooldays, when I had lost one shaft,
I shot his fellow of the self-same flight
The self-same way, with more advisèd watch,
To find the other forth; and by adventuring both
I oft found both. I urge this childhood proof
Because what follows is pure innocence.
I owe you much, and like a wilful youth,
That which I owe is lost; but if you please
To shoot another arrow that self way
Which you did shoot the first, I do not doubt,
150 As I will watch the aim, or to find both
Or bring your latter hazard back again
And thankfully rest debtor for the first.

ANTONIO

You know me well, and herein spend but time
To wind about my love with circumstance;
And out of doubt you do me now more wrong
In making question of my uttermost
Than if you had made waste of all I have.
Then do but say to me what I should do
That in your knowledge may by me be done,
160 And I am prest unto it. Therefore speak.

BASSANIO

In Belmont is a lady richly left,
And she is fair, and, fairer than that word,
Of wondrous virtues. Sometimes from her eyes
I did receive fair speechless messages.
Her name is Portia, nothing undervalued
To Cato's daughter, Brutus' Portia;
Nor is the wide world ignorant of her worth,
For the four winds blow in from every coast

Renownèd suitors, and her sunny locks
Hang on her temples like a golden fleece,   170
Which makes her seat of Belmont Colchos' strond,
And many Jasons come in quest of her.
O my Antonio, had I but the means
To hold a rival place with one of them,
I have a mind presages me such thrift
That I should questionless be fortunate.

ANTONIO
Thou know'st that all my fortunes are at sea,
Neither have I money, nor commodity
To raise a present sum. Therefore go forth;
Try what my credit can in Venice do,   180
That shall be racked even to the uttermost
To furnish thee to Belmont, to fair Portia.
Go presently inquire, and so will I,
Where money is; and I no question make
To have it of my trust or for my sake.   *Exeunt*

    Enter Portia with her waiting-woman, Nerissa   I.2
PORTIA By my troth, Nerissa, my little body is aweary of
  this great world.
NERISSA You would be, sweet madam, if your miseries
  were in the same abundance as your good fortunes are;
  and yet for aught I see, they are as sick that surfeit with
  too much as they that starve with nothing. It is no mean
  happiness, therefore, to be seated in the mean; superfluity comes sooner by white hairs, but competency lives
  longer.
PORTIA Good sentences, and well pronounced.   10
NERISSA They would be better if well followed.
PORTIA If to do were as easy as to know what were good
  to do, chapels had been churches, and poor men's

75

cottages princes' palaces. It is a good divine that follows
his own instructions. I can easier teach twenty what were
good to be done than to be one of the twenty to follow
mine own teaching. The brain may devise laws for the
blood, but a hot temper leaps o'er a cold decree, such a
hare is madness the youth to skip o'er the meshes of good
counsel the cripple. But this reasoning is not in the
fashion to choose me a husband. O me, the word
'choose'! I may neither choose who I would nor refuse
who I dislike, so is the will of a living daughter curbed
by the will of a dead father. Is it not hard, Nerissa, that I
cannot choose one, nor refuse none?

NERISSA Your father was ever virtuous, and holy men at
their death have good inspirations. Therefore the lottery
that he hath devised in these three chests of gold, silver,
and lead, whereof who chooses his meaning chooses you,
will no doubt never be chosen by any rightly but one
who you shall rightly love. But what warmth is there in
your affection towards any of these princely suitors that
are already come?

PORTIA I pray thee overname them, and as thou namest
them I will describe them, and according to my description level at my affection.

NERISSA First, there is the Neapolitan prince.

PORTIA Ay, that's a colt indeed, for he doth nothing but
talk of his horse, and he makes it a great appropriation to
his own good parts that he can shoe him himself. I am
much afeard my lady his mother played false with a
smith.

NERISSA Then is there the County Palatine.

PORTIA He doth nothing but frown, as who should say,
'An you will not have me, choose.' He hears merry tales
and smiles not. I fear he will prove the weeping philosopher when he grows old, being so full of unmannerly

sadness in his youth. I had rather be married to a death's-head with a bone in his mouth than to either of these. God defend me from these two!　　　　　50

NERISSA How say you by the French lord, Monsieur Le Bon?

PORTIA God made him and therefore let him pass for a man. In truth, I know it is a sin to be a mocker, but he, why he hath a horse better than the Neapolitan's, a better bad habit of frowning than the Count Palatine; he is every man in no man. If a throstle sing, he falls straight a-capering; he will fence with his own shadow. If I should marry him, I should marry twenty husbands. If he would despise me, I would forgive him, for if he love　60 me to madness, I shall never requite him.

NERISSA What say you then to Falconbridge, the young baron of England?

PORTIA You know I say nothing to him, for he understands not me, nor I him. He hath neither Latin, French, nor Italian, and you will come into the court and swear that I have a poor pennyworth in the English. He is a proper man's picture, but alas, who can converse with a dumb-show? How oddly he is suited! I think he bought his doublet in Italy, his round hose in France, his bonnet　70 in Germany, and his behaviour everywhere.

NERISSA What think you of the Scottish lord, his neighbour?

PORTIA That he hath a neighbourly charity in him, for he borrowed a box of the ear of the Englishman and swore he would pay him again when he was able. I think the Frenchman became his surety and sealed under for another.

NERISSA How like you the young German, the Duke of Saxony's nephew?　　　　　80

PORTIA Very vilely in the morning when he is sober and

most vilely in the afternoon when he is drunk. When he is best he is a little worse than a man, and when he is worst he is little better than a beast. An the worst fall that ever fell, I hope I shall make shift to go without him.

NERISSA If he should offer to choose, and choose the right casket, you should refuse to perform your father's will if you should refuse to accept him.

PORTIA Therefore, for fear of the worst, I pray thee set a
90 deep glass of Rhenish wine on the contrary casket, for if the devil be within and that temptation without, I know he will choose it. I will do anything, Nerissa, ere I will be married to a sponge.

NERISSA You need not fear, lady, the having any of these lords. They have acquainted me with their determinations, which is indeed to return to their home and to trouble you with no more suit, unless you may be won by some other sort than your father's imposition, depending on the caskets.

100 PORTIA If I live to be as old as Sibylla, I will die as chaste as Diana unless I be obtained by the manner of my father's will. I am glad this parcel of wooers are so reasonable, for there is not one among them but I dote on his very absence, and I pray God grant them a fair departure.

NERISSA Do you not remember, lady, in your father's time, a Venetian, a scholar and a soldier, that came hither in company of the Marquis of Montferrat?

PORTIA Yes, yes, it was Bassanio, as I think, so was he
110 called.

NERISSA True, madam. He, of all the men that ever my foolish eyes looked upon, was the best deserving a fair lady.

PORTIA I remember him well, and I remember him worthy of thy praise.

Enter a Servingman

How now, what news?

SERVINGMAN The four strangers seek for you, madam, to take their leave, and there is a forerunner come from a fifth, the Prince of Morocco, who brings word the Prince his master will be here tonight.   120

PORTIA If I could bid the fifth welcome with so good heart as I can bid the other four farewell, I should be glad of his approach. If he have the condition of a saint and the complexion of a devil, I had rather he should shrive me than wive me. Come, Nerissa. Sirrah, go before. Whiles we shut the gate upon one wooer, another knocks at the door.   *Exeunt*

Enter Bassanio with Shylock the Jew   I.3

SHYLOCK Three thousand ducats, well.

BASSANIO Ay, sir, for three months.

SHYLOCK For three months, well.

BASSANIO For the which, as I told you, Antonio shall be bound.

SHYLOCK Antonio shall become bound, well.

BASSANIO May you stead me? Will you pleasure me? Shall I know your answer?

SHYLOCK Three thousand ducats for three months, and Antonio bound.   10

BASSANIO Your answer to that.

SHYLOCK Antonio is a good man.

BASSANIO Have you heard any imputation to the contrary?

SHYLOCK Ho no, no, no, no! My meaning in saying he is a good man is to have you understand me that he is sufficient. Yet his means are in supposition. He hath an argosy bound to Tripolis, another to the Indies; I

understand, moreover, upon the Rialto, he hath a third
at Mexico, a fourth for England, and other ventures he
hath squandered abroad. But ships are but boards,
sailors but men; there be land rats and water rats, water
thieves and land thieves, I mean pirates; and then there
is the peril of waters, winds, and rocks. The man is, notwithstanding, sufficient. Three thousand ducats; I think
I may take his bond.

BASSANIO Be assured you may.

SHYLOCK I will be assured I may; and that I may be
assured, I will bethink me. May I speak with Antonio?

BASSANIO If it please you to dine with us.

SHYLOCK Yes, to smell pork, to eat of the habitation
which your prophet the Nazarite conjured the devil into.
I will buy with you, sell with you, talk with you, walk
with you, and so following; but I will not eat with you,
drink with you, nor pray with you. What news on the
Rialto? Who is he comes here?

Enter Antonio

BASSANIO
This is Signor Antonio.

SHYLOCK (*aside*)
How like a fawning publican he looks.
I hate him for he is a Christian;
But more, for that in low simplicity
He lends out money gratis and brings down
The rate of usance here with us in Venice.
If I can catch him once upon the hip,
I will feed fat the ancient grudge I bear him.
He hates our sacred nation and he rails
Even there where merchants most do congregate
On me, my bargains, and my well-won thrift,
Which he calls interest. Cursèd be my tribe
If I forgive him.

80

BASSANIO   Shylock, do you hear?

SHYLOCK

  I am debating of my present store,   50
  And by the near guess of my memory
  I cannot instantly raise up the gross
  Of full three thousand ducats. What of that?
  Tubal, a wealthy Hebrew of my tribe,
  Will furnish me. But soft, how many months
  Do you desire? (*To Antonio*) Rest you fair, good signor!
  Your worship was the last man in our mouths.

ANTONIO

  Shylock, albeit I neither lend nor borrow
  By taking nor by giving of excess,
  Yet to supply the ripe wants of my friend,   60
  I'll break a custom. (*To Bassanio*) Is he yet possessed
  How much ye would?

SHYLOCK   Ay, ay, three thousand ducats.

ANTONIO

  And for three months.

SHYLOCK

  I had forgot – three months, you told me so.
  Well then, your bond. And let me see; but hear you,
  Methoughts you said you neither lend nor borrow
  Upon advantage.

ANTONIO   I do never use it.

SHYLOCK

  When Jacob grazed his uncle Laban's sheep –
  This Jacob from our holy Abram was,
  As his wise mother wrought in his behalf,   70
  The third possessor; ay, he was the third –

ANTONIO

  And what of him? Did he take interest?

SHYLOCK

  No, not take interest, not as you would say

Directly interest. Mark what Jacob did:
When Laban and himself were compromised
That all the eanlings which were streaked and pied
Should fall as Jacob's hire, the ewes being rank,
In end of autumn turnèd to the rams;
And when the work of generation was
80   Between these woolly breeders in the act,
The skilful shepherd peeled me certain wands,
And in the doing of the deed of kind
He stuck them up before the fulsome ewes,
Who then conceiving, did in eaning time
Fall parti-coloured lambs, and those were Jacob's.
This was a way to thrive, and he was blest,
And thrift is blessing if men steal it not.

ANTONIO

This was a venture, sir, that Jacob served for,
A thing not in his power to bring to pass,
90   But swayed and fashioned by the hand of heaven.
Was this inserted to make interest good?
Or is your gold and silver ewes and rams?

SHYLOCK

I cannot tell, I make it breed as fast.
But note me, signor –

ANTONIO   Mark you this, Bassanio,
The devil can cite Scripture for his purpose.
An evil soul producing holy witness
Is like a villain with a smiling cheek,
A goodly apple rotten at the heart.
O what a goodly outside falsehood hath!

SHYLOCK

100   Three thousand ducats, 'tis a good round sum.
Three months from twelve, then let me see, the rate . . .

ANTONIO

Well, Shylock, shall we be beholding to you?

SHYLOCK

Signor Antonio, many a time and oft
In the Rialto you have rated me
About my moneys and my usances.
Still have I borne it with a patient shrug,
For sufferance is the badge of all our tribe.
You call me misbeliever, cut-throat dog,
And spit upon my Jewish gaberdine,
And all for use of that which is mine own.   110
Well then, it now appears you need my help.
Go to then. You come to me and you say,
'Shylock, we would have moneys,' you say so,
You, that did void your rheum upon my beard
And foot me as you spurn a stranger cur
Over your threshold, moneys is your suit
What should I say to you? Should I not say,
'Hath a dog money? Is it possible
A cur can lend three thousand ducats?' Or
Shall I bend low, and in a bondman's key,   120
With bated breath and whispering humbleness,
Say this:
'Fair sir, you spat on me on Wednesday last,
You spurned me such a day, another time
You called me dog, and for these courtesies
I'll lend you thus much moneys'?

ANTONIO

I am as like to call thee so again,
To spit on thee again, to spurn thee too.
If thou wilt lend this money, lend it not
As to thy friends, for when did friendship take   130
A breed of barren metal of his friend?
But lend it rather to thine enemy,
Who if he break, thou mayst with better face
Exact the penalty.

83

SHYLOCK Why look you, how you storm!
I would be friends with you and have your love,
Forget the shames that you have stained me with,
Supply your present wants, and take no doit
Of usance for my moneys, and you'll not hear me.
This is kind I offer.

BASSANIO
140 This were kindness.

SHYLOCK This kindness will I show.
Go with me to a notary, seal me there
Your single bond, and, in a merry sport,
If you repay me not on such a day,
In such a place, such sum or sums as are
Expressed in the condition, let the forfeit
Be nominated for an equal pound
Of your fair flesh, to be cut off and taken
In what part of your body pleaseth me.

ANTONIO
Content, in faith. I'll seal to such a bond
150 And say there is much kindness in the Jew.

BASSANIO
You shall not seal to such a bond for me;
I'll rather dwell in my necessity.

ANTONIO
Why fear not, man; I will not forfeit it.
Within these two months – that's a month before
This bond expires – I do expect return
Of thrice three times the value of this bond.

SHYLOCK
O father Abram, what these Christians are,
Whose own hard dealings teaches them suspect
The thoughts of others! Pray you tell me this:
160 If he should break his day, what should I gain
By the exaction of the forfeiture?

84

A pound of man's flesh taken from a man
Is not so estimable, profitable neither,
As flesh of muttons, beefs, or goats. I say
To buy his favour I extend this friendship.
If he will take it, so; if not, adieu.
And for my love I pray you wrong me not.

ANTONIO

Yes, Shylock, I will seal unto this bond.

SHYLOCK

Then meet me forthwith at the notary's;
Give him direction for this merry bond,   170
And I will go and purse the ducats straight,
See to my house, left in the fearful guard
Of an unthrifty knave, and presently
I'll be with you.   *Exit*

ANTONIO   Hie thee, gentle Jew.
The Hebrew will turn Christian; he grows kind.

BASSANIO

I like not fair terms and a villain's mind.

ANTONIO

Come on. In this there can be no dismay;
My ships come home a month before the day. *Exeunt*

*

Flourish of cornets. Enter the Prince of Morocco, a   **II.1**
tawny Moor all in white, and three or four followers
accordingly, with Portia, Nerissa, and their train

MOROCCO

Mislike me not for my complexion,
The shadowed livery of the burnished sun,
To whom I am a neighbour and near bred.
Bring me the fairest creature northward born,

Where Phoebus' fire scarce thaws the icicles,
And let us make incision for your love
To prove whose blood is reddest, his or mine.
I tell thee, lady, this aspect of mine
Hath feared the valiant. By my love I swear,
The best-regarded virgins of our clime
Have loved it too. I would not change this hue,
Except to steal your thoughts, my gentle queen.

PORTIA

In terms of choice I am not solely led
By nice direction of a maiden's eyes.
Besides, the lott'ry of my destiny
Bars me the right of voluntary choosing.
But if my father had not scanted me,
And hedged me by his wit to yield myself
His wife who wins me by that means I told you,
Yourself, renownèd Prince, then stood as fair
As any comer I have looked on yet
For my affection.

MOROCCO   Even for that I thank you.

Therefore I pray you lead me to the caskets
To try my fortune. By this scimitar
That slew the Sophy and a Persian prince
That won three fields of Sultan Solyman,
I would o'erstare the sternest eyes that look,
Outbrave the heart most daring on the earth,
Pluck the young sucking cubs from the she-bear,
Yea, mock the lion when 'a roars for prey,
To win thee, lady. But alas the while,
If Hercules and Lichas play at dice
Which is the better man, the greater throw
May turn by fortune from the weaker hand.
So is Alcides beaten by his page,
And so may I, blind Fortune leading me,

Miss that which one unworthier may attain,
And die with grieving.

PORTIA   You must take your chance,
And either not attempt to choose at all
Or swear before you choose, if you choose wrong   40
Never to speak to lady afterward
In way of marriage. Therefore be advised.

MOROCCO

Nor will not. Come, bring me unto my chance.

PORTIA

First, forward to the temple; after dinner
Your hazard shall be made.

MOROCCO   Good fortune then,
To make me blest or cursèd'st among men!

Flourish of cornets. Exeunt

Enter Launcelot Gobbo, alone   II.2

LAUNCELOT Certainly my conscience will serve me to run
from this Jew my master. The fiend is at mine elbow and
tempts me, saying to me, 'Gobbo, Launcelot Gobbo,
good Launcelot,' or 'Good Gobbo,' or 'Good Launcelot
Gobbo, use your legs, take the start, run away.' My conscience says, 'No, take heed, honest Launcelot, take
heed, honest Gobbo,' or as aforesaid, 'Honest Launcelot
Gobbo, do not run, scorn running with thy heels.' Well,
the most courageous fiend bids me pack. 'Fia!' says the
fiend; 'Away!' says the fiend. 'For the heavens, rouse up a   10
brave mind,' says the fiend, 'and run.' Well, my conscience hanging about the neck of my heart says very
wisely to me, 'My honest friend Launcelot', being an
honest man's son or rather an honest woman's son, for
indeed my father did something smack, something grow
to, he had a kind of taste – well, my conscience says,

87

'Launcelot, budge not.' 'Budge,' says the fiend. 'Budge
not,' says my conscience. 'Conscience,' say I, 'you counsel well.' 'Fiend,' say I, 'you counsel well.' To be ruled
20   by my conscience, I should stay with the Jew my master
who, God bless the mark, is a kind of devil; and to run
away from the Jew, I should be ruled by the fiend, who,
saving your reverence, is the devil himself. Certainly the
Jew is the very devil incarnation; and in my conscience,
my conscience is but a kind of hard conscience to offer to
counsel me to stay with the Jew. The fiend gives the
more friendly counsel. I will run, fiend; my heels are at
your commandment; I will run.

Enter Old Gobbo with a basket

GOBBO Master young man, you I pray you, which is the
30   way to Master Jew's?

LAUNCELOT (*aside*) O heavens, this is my true-begotten
father who, being more than sand-blind, high-gravel-
blind, knows me not. I will try confusions with him.

GOBBO Master young gentleman, I pray you which is the
way to Master Jew's?

LAUNCELOT Turn up on your right hand at the next turning, but at the next turning of all, on your left, marry, at
the very next turning turn of no hand, but turn down
indirectly to the Jew's house.

40   GOBBO By God's sonties, 'twill be a hard way to hit! Can
you tell me whether one Launcelot that dwells with him,
dwell with him or no?

LAUNCELOT Talk you of young Master Launcelot?
(*aside*) Mark me now, now will I raise the waters. – Talk
you of young Master Launcelot?

GOBBO No master, sir, but a poor man's son. His father,
though I say't, is an honest exceeding poor man and,
God be thanked, well to live.

LAUNCELOT Well, let his father be what 'a will, we talk of
50   young Master Launcelot.

GOBBO Your worship's friend, and Launcelot, sir.

LAUNCELOT But I pray you, ergo old man, ergo I beseech you, talk you of young Master Launcelot.

GOBBO Of Launcelot, an't please your mastership.

LAUNCELOT Ergo, Master Launcelot. Talk not of Master Launcelot, father, for the young gentleman, according to Fates and Destinies and such odd sayings, the Sisters Three and such branches of learning, is indeed deceased, or as you would say in plain terms, gone to heaven.

GOBBO Marry, God forbid! The boy was the very staff of 60 my age, my very prop.

LAUNCELOT Do I look like a cudgel or a hovel-post, a staff or a prop? Do you know me, father?

GOBBO Alack the day, I know you not, young gentleman! But I pray you tell me, is my boy, God rest his soul, alive or dead?

LAUNCELOT Do you not know me, father?

GOBBO Alack, sir, I am sand-blind! I know you not.

LAUNCELOT Nay, indeed if you had your eyes you might fail of the knowing me; it is a wise father that knows his 70 own child. Well, old man, I will tell you news of your son. (*He kneels*) Give me your blessing. Truth will come to light; murder cannot be hid long – a man's son may, but in the end truth will out.

GOBBO Pray you, sir, stand up. I am sure you are not Launcelot my boy.

LAUNCELOT Pray you let's have no more fooling about it, but give me your blessing. I am Launcelot, your boy that was, your son that is, your child that shall be.

GOBBO I cannot think you are my son. 80

LAUNCELOT I know not what I shall think of that; but I am Launcelot, the Jew's man, and I am sure Margery your wife is my mother.

GOBBO Her name is Margery indeed. I'll be sworn, if thou be Launcelot thou art mine own flesh and blood. Lord

89

worshipped might he be, what a beard hast thou got!
Thou hast got more hair on thy chin than Dobbin my
fill-horse has on his tail.

LAUNCELOT It should seem then that Dobbin's tail grows
backward. I am sure he had more hair on his tail than I
have on my face when I last saw him.

GOBBO Lord, how art thou changed! How dost thou and
thy master agree? I have brought him a present. How
'gree you now?

LAUNCELOT Well, well; but for mine own part, as I have
set up my rest to run away, so I will not rest till I have
run some ground. My master's a very Jew. Give him a
present? Give him a halter! I am famished in his service;
you may tell every finger I have with my ribs. Father, I
am glad you are come. Give me your present to one
Master Bassanio, who indeed gives rare new liveries. If
I serve not him, I will run as far as God has any ground.
O rare fortune, here comes the man! To him, father, for
I am a Jew if I serve the Jew any longer.

Enter Bassanio, with Leonardo and a follower or two

BASSANIO You may do so, but let it be so hasted that supper be ready at the farthest by five of the clock. See these
letters delivered, put the liveries to making, and desire
Gratiano to come anon to my lodging.

Exit one of his men

LAUNCELOT To him, father!

GOBBO God bless your worship!

BASSANIO Gramercy. Wouldst thou aught with me?

GOBBO Here's my son, sir, a poor boy . . .

LAUNCELOT Not a poor boy, sir, but the rich Jew's man
that would, sir, as my father shall specify . . .

GOBBO He hath a great infection, sir, as one would say,
to serve . . .

LAUNCELOT Indeed, the short and the long is, I serve the

Jew, and have a desire, as my father shall specify ...

GOBBO His master and he, saving your worship's reverence, are scarce cater-cousins.   120

LAUNCELOT To be brief, the very truth is that the Jew having done me wrong doth cause me, as my father, being I hope an old man, shall frutify unto you ...

GOBBO I have here a dish of doves that I would bestow upon your worship, and my suit is ...

LAUNCELOT In very brief, the suit is impertinent to myself, as your worship shall know by this honest old man, and though I say it, though old man, yet poor man, my father ...

BASSANIO One speak for both. What would you?   130

LAUNCELOT Serve you, sir.

GOBBO That is the very defect of the matter, sir.

BASSANIO
I know thee well, thou hast obtained thy suit.
Shylock thy master spoke with me this day,
And hath preferred thee, if it be preferment
To leave a rich Jew's service to become
The follower of so poor a gentleman.

LAUNCELOT The old proverb is very well parted between my master Shylock and you, sir. You have the grace of God, sir, and he hath enough.   140

BASSANIO
Thou speak'st it well. Go, father, with thy son;
Take leave of thy old master and inquire
My lodging out. (*To a Servant*) Give him a livery
More guarded than his fellows'. See it done.

LAUNCELOT Father, in. I cannot get a service, no! I have ne'er a tongue in my head, well! (*He looks at his palm*) If any man in Italy have a fairer table which doth offer to swear upon a book, I shall have good fortune! Go to, here's a simple line of life. Here's a small trifle of wives!

150 Alas, fifteen wives is nothing; eleven widows and nine
maids is a simple coming-in for one man. And then to
scape drowning thrice, and to be in peril of my life with
the edge of a feather-bed! Here are simple scapes. Well,
if Fortune be a woman, she's a good wench for this gear.
Father, come. I'll take my leave of the Jew in the twinkling.   *Exit Launcelot, with old Gobbo*

BASSANIO

I pray thee, good Leonardo, think on this.
These things being bought and orderly bestowed,
Return in haste, for I do feast tonight
160 My best-esteemed acquaintance. Hie thee, go.

LEONARDO

My best endeavours shall be done herein.
        Enter Gratiano

GRATIANO

Where's your master?

LEONARDO   Yonder, sir, he walks.   *Exit*

GRATIANO

Signor Bassanio!

BASSANIO

Gratiano!

GRATIANO

I have suit to you.

BASSANIO   You have obtained it.

GRATIANO

You must not deny me. I must go with you to Belmont.

BASSANIO

Why then you must. But hear thee, Gratiano:
Thou art too wild, too rude and bold of voice,
Parts that become thee happily enough
170 And in such eyes as ours appear not faults,
But where thou art not known, why there they show
Something too liberal. Pray thee take pain

92

To allay with some cold drops of modesty
Thy skipping spirit, lest through thy wild behaviour
I be misconstered in the place I go to,
And lose my hopes.

GRATIANO   Signor Bassanio, hear me:
If I do not put on a sober habit,
Talk with respect, and swear but now and then,
Wear prayer books in my pocket, look demurely,
Nay more, while grace is saying hood mine eyes   180
Thus with my hat, and sigh and say amen,
Use all the observance of civility
Like one well studied in a sad ostent
To please his grandam, never trust me more.

BASSANIO
Well, we shall see your bearing.

GRATIANO
Nay, but I bar tonight. You shall not gauge me
By what we do tonight.

BASSANIO   No, that were pity.
I would entreat you rather to put on
Your boldest suit of mirth, for we have friends
That purpose merriment. But fare you well;   190
I have some business.

GRATIANO
And I must to Lorenzo and the rest,
But we will visit you at supper-time.   *Exeunt*

Enter Jessica and Launcelot the Clown   II.3
JESSICA
I am sorry thou wilt leave my father so.
Our house is hell, and thou a merry devil
Didst rob it of some taste of tediousness.
But fare thee well, there is a ducat for thee.

And, Launcelot, soon at supper shalt thou see
Lorenzo, who is thy new master's guest.
Give him this letter; do it secretly.
And so farewell; I would not have my father
See me in talk with thee.

10   LAUNCELOT Adieu! Tears exhibit my tongue. Most beautiful pagan, most sweet Jew! If a Christian did not play the knave and get thee, I am much deceived. But adieu. These foolish drops do something drown my manly spirit. Adieu!

JESSICA
Farewell, good Launcelot.   *Exit Launcelot*
Alack, what heinous sin is it in me
To be ashamed to be my father's child.
But though I am a daughter to his blood,
I am not to his manners. O Lorenzo, .
20   If thou keep promise, I shall end this strife,
Become a Christian and thy loving wife.

II.4   *Enter Gratiano, Lorenzo, Salerio, and Solanio*

LORENZO
Nay, we will slink away in supper-time,
Disguise us at my lodging, and return
All in an hour.

GRATIANO
We have not made good preparation.

SALERIO
We have not spoke us yet of torchbearers.

SOLANIO
'Tis vile, unless it may be quaintly ordered,
And better in my mind not undertook.

LORENZO
'Tis now but four of clock. We have two hours

To furnish us.

Enter Launcelot with a letter

Friend Launcelot, what's the news?

LAUNCELOT An it shall please you to break up this, it 10
shall seem to signify.

LORENZO

I know the hand. In faith, 'tis a fair hand,
And whiter than the paper it writ on
Is the fair hand that writ.

GRATIANO Love-news, in faith!

LAUNCELOT By your leave, sir.

LORENZO Whither goest thou?

LAUNCELOT Marry, sir, to bid my old master the Jew to
sup tonight with my new master the Christian.

LORENZO

Hold here, take this. (*Gives money*) Tell gentle Jessica
I will not fail her. Speak it privately.   *Exit Launcelot* 20
Go, gentlemen;
Will you prepare you for this masque tonight?
I am provided of a torchbearer.

SALERIO

Ay marry, I'll be gone about it straight.

SOLANIO

And so will I.

LORENZO   Meet me and Gratiano
At Gratiano's lodging some hour hence.

SALERIO

'Tis good we do so.   *Exit with Solanio*

GRATIANO

Was not that letter from fair Jessica?

LORENZO

I must needs tell thee all. She hath directed
How I shall take her from her father's house,   30
What gold and jewels she is furnished with,

95

What page's suit she hath in readiness.
If e'er the Jew her father come to heaven,
It will be for his gentle daughter's sake;
And never dare misfortune cross her foot,
Unless she do it under this excuse,
That she is issue to a faithless Jew.
Come, go with me; peruse this as thou goest.
Fair Jessica shall be my torchbearer. *Exit with Gratiano*

II.5   *Enter Shylock the Jew and Launcelot, his man that
             was, the Clown*

SHYLOCK
Well, thou shalt see, thy eyes shall be thy judge,
The difference of old Shylock and Bassanio. . . .
What, Jessica! Thou shalt not gormandize
As thou hast done with me . . . What, Jessica! . . .
And sleep, and snore, and rend apparel out . . .
Why, Jessica, I say!
LAUNCELOT   Why, Jessica!
SHYLOCK
Who bids thee call? I do not bid thee call.
LAUNCELOT Your worship was wont to tell me I could do
nothing without bidding.
         Enter Jessica
JESSICA
10   Call you? What is your will?
SHYLOCK
I am bid forth to supper, Jessica.
There are my keys. But wherefore should I go?
I am not bid for love, they flatter me,
But yet I'll go in hate to feed upon
The prodigal Christian. Jessica my girl,
Look to my house. I am right loath to go.

There is some ill a-brewing towards my rest,
For I did dream of money bags tonight.

LAUNCELOT I beseech you, sir, go. My young master
doth expect your reproach.   20

SHYLOCK So do I his.

LAUNCELOT And they have conspired together. I will not
say you shall see a masque, but if you do, then it was not
for nothing that my nose fell a-bleeding on Black Monday last at six o'clock i'th'morning, falling out that year
on Ash Wednesday was four year in th'afternoon.

SHYLOCK
What, are there masques? Hear you me, Jessica:
Lock up my doors; and when you hear the drum
And the vile squealing of the wry-necked fife,
Clamber not you up to the casements then,   30
Nor thrust your head into the public street
To gaze on Christian fools with varnished faces;
But stop my house's ears, I mean my casements;
Let not the sound of shallow foppery enter
My sober house. By Jacob's staff I swear
I have no mind of feasting forth tonight,
But I will go. Go you before me, sirrah.
Say I will come.

LAUNCELOT   I will go before, sir.
Mistress, look out at window for all this:
There will come a Christian by   40
Will be worth a Jewess' eye.   *Exit*

SHYLOCK
What says that fool of Hagar's offspring, ha?

JESSICA
His words were 'Farewell, mistress', nothing else.

SHYLOCK
The patch is kind enough, but a huge feeder,
Snail-slow in profit, and he sleeps by day

97

More than the wildcat. Drones hive not with me;
Therefore I part with him, and part with him
To one that I would have him help to waste
His borrowed purse. Well, Jessica, go in.
50 Perhaps I will return immediately.
Do as I bid you; shut doors after you.
Fast bind, fast find,
A proverb never stale in thrifty mind.   *Exit*

JESSICA
Farewell; and if my fortune be not crost,
I have a father, you a daughter, lost.   *Exit*

II.6   *Enter the masquers, Gratiano and Salerio*

GRATIANO
This is the penthouse under which Lorenzo
Desired us to make stand.

SALERIO   His hour is almost past.

GRATIANO
And it is marvel he outdwells his hour,
For lovers ever run before the clock.

SALERIO
O ten times faster Venus' pigeons fly
To seal love's bonds new-made than they are wont
To keep obligèd faith unforfeited!

GRATIANO
That ever holds. Who riseth from a feast
With that keen appetite that he sits down?
10 Where is the horse that doth untread again
His tedious measures with the unbated fire
That he did pace them first? All things that are
Are with more spirit chasèd than enjoyed.
How like a younger or a prodigal
The scarfèd bark puts from her native bay,

98

Hugged and embracèd by the strumpet wind.
How like the prodigal doth she return,
With overweathered ribs and ragged sails,
Lean, rent, and beggared by the strumpet wind.

Enter Lorenzo

SALERIO

Here comes Lorenzo; more of this hereafter.   20

LORENZO

Sweet friends, your patience for my long abode.
Not I but my affairs have made you wait.
When you shall please to play the thieves for wives,
I'll watch as long for you then. Approach.
Here dwells my father Jew. Ho! Who's within?

Enter Jessica above, in boy's clothes

JESSICA

Who are you? Tell me for more certainty,
Albeit I'll swear that I do know your tongue.

LORENZO

Lorenzo, and thy love.

JESSICA

Lorenzo certain, and my love indeed,
For who love I so much? And now who knows   30
But you, Lorenzo, whether I am yours?

LORENZO

Heaven and thy thoughts are witness that thou art.

JESSICA

Here, catch this casket; it is worth the pains.
I am glad 'tis night, you do not look on me,
For I am much ashamed of my exchange.
But love is blind, and lovers cannot see
The pretty follies that themselves commit;
For if they could, Cupid himself would blush
To see me thus transformèd to a boy.

LORENZO

40   Descend, for you must be my torchbearer.

JESSICA

What, must I hold a candle to my shames?
They in themselves, good sooth, are too too light.
Why, 'tis an office of discovery, love,
And I should be obscured.

LORENZO   So are you, sweet,
Even in the lovely garnish of a boy.
But come at once,
For the close night doth play the runaway,
And we are stayed for at Bassanio's feast.

JESSICA

I will make fast the doors, and gild myself
50   With some more ducats, and be with you straight.

                           Exit above

GRATIANO

Now by my hood, a gentle and no Jew!

LORENZO

Beshrew me but I love her heartily!
For she is wise, if I can judge of her,
And fair she is, if that mine eyes be true,
And true she is, as she hath proved herself;
And therefore, like herself, wise, fair, and true,
Shall she be placèd in my constant soul.

    Enter Jessica below

What, art thou come? On, gentlemen, away!
Our masquing mates by this time for us stay.

                Exit with Jessica and Salerio

    Enter Antonio

ANTONIO

60   Who's there?

GRATIANO

Signor Antonio?

ANTONIO

Fie, fie, Gratiano! Where are all the rest?
'Tis nine o'clock; our friends all stay for you.
No masque tonight. The wind is come about;
Bassanio presently will go aboard.
I have sent twenty out to seek for you.

GRATIANO

I am glad on't. I desire no more delight
Than to be under sail and gone tonight.   *Exeunt*

Flourish of cornets. Enter Portia with Morocco and II.7
both their trains

PORTIA

Go, draw aside the curtains and discover
The several caskets to this noble Prince.
Now make your choice.

MOROCCO

This first, of gold, who this inscription bears,
Who chooseth me shall gain what many men desire;
The second, silver, which this promise carries,
Who chooseth me shall get as much as he deserves;
This third, dull lead, with warning all as blunt,
Who chooseth me must give and hazard all he hath.
How shall I know if I do choose the right?   10

PORTIA

The one of them contains my picture, Prince.
If you choose that, then I am yours withal.

MOROCCO

Some god direct my judgement! Let me see:
I will survey th'inscriptions back again.
What says this leaden casket?
Who chooseth me must give and hazard all he hath.
Must give, for what? For lead! Hazard for lead?

This casket threatens; men that hazard all
Do it in hope of fair advantages.
20 A golden mind stoops not to shows of dross;
I'll then nor give nor hazard aught for lead.
What says the silver with her virgin hue?
Who chooseth me shall get as much as he deserves.
As much as he deserves? Pause there, Morocco,
And weigh thy value with an even hand.
If thou be'st rated by thy estimation,
Thou dost deserve enough and yet enough
May not extend so far as to the lady,
And yet to be afeard of my deserving
30 Were but a weak disabling of myself.
As much as I deserve? Why that's the lady!
I do in birth deserve her, and in fortunes,
In graces, and in qualities of breeding;
But more than these, in love I do deserve.
What if I strayed no farther, but chose here?
Let's see once more this saying graved in gold:
Who chooseth me shall gain what many men desire.
Why that's the lady! All the world desires her;
From the four corners of the earth they come
40 To kiss this shrine, this mortal breathing saint.
The Hyrcanian deserts and the vasty wilds
Of wide Arabia are as throughfares now
For princes to come view fair Portia.
The watery kingdom, whose ambitious head
Spits in the face of heaven, is no bar
To stop the foreign spirits, but they come
As o'er a brook to see fair Portia.
One of these three contains her heavenly picture.
Is't like that lead contains her? 'Twere damnation
50 To think so base a thought; it were too gross
To rib her cerecloth in the obscure grave.

Or shall I think in silver she's immured,
Being ten times undervalued to tried gold?
O sinful thought! Never so rich a gem
Was set in worse than gold. They have in England
A coin that bears the figure of an angel
Stampèd in gold – but that's insculped upon;
But here an angel in a golden bed
Lies all within. Deliver me the key.
Here do I choose, and thrive I as I may!   60

PORTIA

There, take it, Prince, and if my form lie there,
Then I am yours.

    He opens the golden casket

MOROCCO   O hell! What have we here?
A carrion Death, within whose empty eye
There is a written scroll. I'll read the writing.

   All that glisters is not gold;
   Often have you heard that told.
   Many a man his life hath sold
   But my outside to behold.
   Gilded tombs do worms infold.
   Had you been as wise as bold,   70
   Young in limbs, in judgement old,
   Your answer had not been inscrolled.
   Fare you well, your suit is cold.
      Cold indeed, and labour lost.
      Then farewell heat, and welcome frost.
Portia, adieu, I have too grieved a heart
To take a tedious leave. Thus losers part.

          Exit with his train. Flourish of cornets

PORTIA

A gentle riddance. Draw the curtains, go.
Let all of his complexion choose me so.   *Exeunt*

SALERIO

Why, man, I saw Bassanio under sail;
With him is Gratiano gone along,
And in their ship I am sure Lorenzo is not.

SOLANIO

The villain Jew with outcries raised the Duke,
Who went with him to search Bassanio's ship.

SALERIO

He came too late, the ship was under sail,
But there the Duke was given to understand
That in a gondola were seen together
Lorenzo and his amorous Jessica.

10   Besides, Antonio certified the Duke
They were not with Bassanio in his ship.

SOLANIO

I never heard a passion so confused,
So strange, outrageous, and so variable
As the dog Jew did utter in the streets:
'My daughter! O my ducats! O my daughter!
Fled with a Christian! O my Christian ducats!
Justice! The law! My ducats and my daughter!
A sealèd bag, two sealèd bags of ducats,
Of double ducats, stol'n from me by my daughter!

20   And jewels, two stones, two rich and precious stones,
Stol'n by my daughter! Justice! Find the girl!
She hath the stones upon her, and the ducats!'

SALERIO

Why, all the boys in Venice follow him,
Crying his stones, his daughter, and his ducats.

SOLANIO

Let good Antonio look he keep his day,
Or he shall pay for this.

SALERIO   Marry, well remembered.

I reasoned with a Frenchman yesterday,
Who told me, in the narrow seas that part
The French and English there miscarrièd
A vessel of our country richly fraught. 30
I thought upon Antonio when he told me,
And wished in silence that it were not his.

SOLANIO

You were best to tell Antonio what you hear,
Yet do not suddenly, for it may grieve him.

SALERIO

A kinder gentleman treads not the earth.
I saw Bassanio and Antonio part;
Bassanio told him he would make some speed
Of his return; he answered, 'Do not so.
Slubber not business for my sake, Bassanio,
But stay the very riping of the time. 40
And for the Jew's bond which he hath of me,
Let it not enter in your mind of love.
Be merry, and employ your chiefest thoughts
To courtship and such fair ostents of love
As shall conveniently become you there.'
And even there, his eye being big with tears,
Turning his face, he put his hand behind him,
And with affection wondrous sensible
He wrung Bassanio's hand; and so they parted.

SOLANIO

I think he only loves the world for him. 50
I pray thee let us go and find him out,
And quicken his embracèd heaviness
With some delight or other.

SALERIO   Do we so.   *Exeunt*

NERISSA

Quick, quick I pray thee! Draw the curtain straight.
The Prince of Arragon hath ta'en his oath,
And comes to his election presently.

Flourish of cornets. Enter Arragon, his train, and Portia

PORTIA

Behold, there stand the caskets, noble Prince.
If you choose that wherein I am contained,
Straight shall our nuptial rites be solemnized;
But if you fail, without more speech, my lord,
You must be gone from hence immediately.

ARRAGON

I am enjoined by oath to observe three things:
First, never to unfold to anyone
Which casket 'twas I chose; next, if I fail
Of the right casket, never in my life
To woo a maid in way of marriage;
Lastly,
If I do fail in fortune of my choice,
Immediately to leave you and be gone.

PORTIA

To these injunctions everyone doth swear
That comes to hazard for my worthless self.

ARRAGON

And so have I addressed me. Fortune now
To my heart's hope! Gold, silver, and base lead.
Who chooseth me must give and hazard all he hath.
You shall look fairer ere I give or hazard.
What says the golden chest? Ha, let me see.
Who chooseth me shall gain what many men desire.
What many men desire; that 'many' may be meant
By the fool multitude that choose by show,
Not learning more than the fond eye doth teach,

Which pries not to th'interior, but like the martlet
Builds in the weather on the outward wall,
Even in the force and road of casualty.⁣   30
I will not choose what many men desire,
Because I will not jump with common spirits
And rank me with the barbarous multitudes.
Why then, to thee, thou silver treasure house.
Tell me once more what title thou dost bear.
Who chooseth me shall get as much as he deserves.
And well said too, for who shall go about
To cozen fortune, and be honourable
Without the stamp of merit? Let none presume
To wear an undeservèd dignity.⁣   40
O that estates, degrees, and offices
Were not derived corruptly, and that clear honour
Were purchased by the merit of the wearer!
How many then should cover that stand bare,
How many be commanded that command;
How much low peasantry would then be gleaned
From the true seed of honour, and how much honour
Picked from the chaff and ruin of the times
To be new varnished. Well, but to my choice.
Who chooseth me shall get as much as he deserves.⁣   50
I will assume desert. Give me a key for this,
And instantly unlock my fortunes here.

    He opens the silver casket

PORTIA

Too long a pause for that which you find there.

ARRAGON

What's here? The portrait of a blinking idiot
Presenting me a schedule! I will read it.
How much unlike art thou to Portia!
How much unlike my hopes and my deservings!
Who chooseth me shall have as much as he deserves.

Did I deserve no more than a fool's head?
60 Is that my prize? Are my deserts no better?

PORTIA
To offend and judge are distinct offices,
And of opposèd natures.

ARRAGON   What is here?
    The fire seven times trièd this;
    Seven times tried that judgement is
    That did never choose amiss.
    Some there be that shadows kiss;
    Such have but a shadow's bliss.
    There be fools alive iwis,
    Silvered o'er, and so was this.
70 *Take what wife you will to bed,*
    I will ever be your head.
    So be gone; you are sped.
    Still more fool I shall appear
    By the time I linger here.
    With one fool's head I came to woo,
    But I go away with two.
    Sweet, adieu. I'll keep my oath,
    Patiently to bear my wroth.   *Exit with his train*

PORTIA
    Thus hath the candle singed the moth.
80 O these deliberate fools! When they do choose,
    They have the wisdom by their wit to lose.

NERISSA
    The ancient saying is no heresy:
    Hanging and wiving goes by destiny.

PORTIA
    Come draw the curtain, Nerissa.
        Enter Messenger

MESSENGER
    Where is my lady?

108

PORTIA   Here. What would my lord?

MESSENGER

Madam, there is alighted at your gate
A young Venetian, one that comes before
To signify th'approaching of his lord,
From whom he bringeth sensible regreets,
To wit, besides commends and courteous breath,   90
Gifts of rich value. Yet I have not seen
So likely an ambassador of love.
A day in April never came so sweet
To show how costly summer was at hand,
As this fore-spurrer comes before his lord.

PORTIA

No more, I pray thee, I am half afeard
Thou wilt say anon he is some kin to thee,
Thou spend'st such high-day wit in praising him.
Come, come, Nerissa, for I long to see
Quick Cupid's post that comes so mannerly.   100

NERISSA

Bassanio Lord, love if thy will it be!   *Exeunt*

✳

Enter Solanio and Salerio   III.1

SOLANIO Now what news on the Rialto?

SALERIO Why, yet it lives there unchecked that Antonio
hath a ship of rich lading wracked on the narrow seas,
the Goodwins I think they call the place, a very dangerous flat, and fatal, where the carcasses of many a tall ship
lie buried as they say, if my gossip Report be an honest
woman of her word.

SOLANIO I would she were as lying a gossip in that as
ever knapped ginger or made her neighbours believe she

109

10   wept for the death of a third husband. But it is true,
without any slips of prolixity or crossing the plain high-
way of talk, that the good Antonio, the honest Antonio –
O that I had a title good enough to keep his name company . . .

SALERIO Come, the full stop!

SOLANIO Ha, what sayest thou? Why the end is, he hath
lost a ship.

SALERIO I would it might prove the end of his losses.

SOLANIO Let me say amen betimes lest the devil cross my
20   prayer, for here he comes in the likeness of a Jew.

    Enter Shylock

How now, Shylock? What news among the merchants?

SHYLOCK You knew, none so well, none so well as you, of
my daughter's flight.

SALERIO That's certain. I for my part knew the tailor
that made the wings she flew withal.

SOLANIO And Shylock for his own part knew the bird was
fledged, and then it is the complexion of them all to
leave the dam.

SHYLOCK She is damned for it.

30 SALERIO That's certain, if the devil may be her judge.

SHYLOCK My own flesh and blood to rebel!

SOLANIO Out upon it, old carrion! Rebels it at these
years?

SHYLOCK I say my daughter is my flesh and my blood.

SALERIO There is more difference between thy flesh and
hers than between jet and ivory, more between your
bloods than there is between red wine and Rhenish. But
tell us, do you hear whether Antonio have had any loss
at sea or no?

40 SHYLOCK There I have another bad match! A bankrupt,
a prodigal, who dare scarce show his head on the Rialto,
a beggar that was used to come so smug upon the mart!

Let him look to his bond. He was wont to call me usurer.
Let him look to his bond. He was wont to lend money
for a Christian courtesy. Let him look to his bond.

SALERIO Why, I am sure if he forfeit thou wilt not take his
flesh. What's that good for?

SHYLOCK To bait fish withal. If it will feed nothing else,
it will feed my revenge. He hath disgraced me and hin-
dered me half a million, laughed at my losses, mocked at 50
my gains, scorned my nation, thwarted my bargains,
cooled my friends, heated mine enemies, and what's his
reason? I am a Jew. Hath not a Jew eyes? Hath not a
Jew hands, organs, dimensions, senses, affections, passions? Fed with the same food, hurt with the same
weapons, subject to the same diseases, healed by the
same means, warmed and cooled by the same winter and
summer as a Christian is? If you prick us, do we not
bleed? If you tickle us, do we not laugh? If you poison
us, do we not die? And if you wrong us, shall we not 60
revenge? If we are like you in the rest, we will resemble
you in that. If a Jew wrong a Christian, what is his
humility? Revenge. If a Christian wrong a Jew, what
should his sufferance be by Christian example? Why,
revenge! The villainy you teach me I will execute, and it
shall go hard but I will better the instruction.

Enter a Man from Antonio

MAN Gentlemen, my master Antonio is at his house and
desires to speak with you both.

SALERIO We have been up and down to seek him.

Enter Tubal

SOLANIO Here comes another of the tribe. A third cannot 70
be matched, unless the devil himself turn Jew.

Exeunt Solanio, Salerio, and Man

SHYLOCK How now, Tubal! What news from Genoa?
Hast thou found my daughter?

TUBAL I often came where I did hear of her, but cannot
find her.

SHYLOCK Why there, there, there, there! A diamond gone
cost me two thousand ducats in Frankfurt! The curse
never fell upon our nation till now; I never felt it till
now. Two thousand ducats in that, and other precious,
80 precious jewels. I would my daughter were dead at my
foot, and the jewels in her ear! Would she were hearsed
at my foot, and the ducats in her coffin! No news of
them, why so? – And I know not what's spent in the
search. Why thou loss upon loss! The thief gone with so
much, and so much to find the thief! – And no satisfac-
tion, no revenge! Nor no ill luck stirring but what lights
o'my shoulders, no sighs but o'my breathing, no tears
but o'my shedding.

TUBAL Yes, other men have ill luck too. Antonio, as I
90 heard in Genoa . . .

SHYLOCK What, what, what? Ill luck, ill luck?

TUBAL Hath an argosy cast away coming from Tripolis.

SHYLOCK I thank God, I thank God! Is it true? Is it true?

TUBAL I spoke with some of the sailors that escaped the
wrack.

SHYLOCK I thank thee, good Tubal. Good news, good
news! Ha, ha! Heard in Genoa?

TUBAL Your daughter spent in Genoa, as I heard, one night
fourscore ducats.

100 **SHYLOCK** Thou stick'st a dagger in me. I shall never see
my gold again. Fourscore ducats at a sitting, fourscore
ducats!

TUBAL There came divers of Antonio's creditors in my
company to Venice that swear he cannot choose but
break.

SHYLOCK I am very glad of it. I'll plague him; I'll torture
him. I am glad of it.

TUBAL One of them showed me a ring that he had of your
daughter for a monkey.

SHYLOCK Out upon her! Thou torturest me, Tubal. It 110
was my turquoise; I had it of Leah when I was a
bachelor. I would not have given it for a wilderness of
monkeys.

TUBAL But Antonio is certainly undone.

SHYLOCK Nay, that's true, that's very true. Go, Tubal,
fee me an officer; bespeak him a fortnight before. I will
have the heart of him if he forfeit, for were he out of
Venice I can make what merchandise I will. Go, Tubal,
and meet me at our synagogue; go, good Tubal; at our
synagogue, Tubal.   *Exeunt* 120

Enter Bassanio, Portia, Gratiano, Nerissa, and all III.2
their trains

PORTIA

I pray you tarry, pause a day or two
Before you hazard, for in choosing wrong
I lose your company. Therefore forbear awhile.
There's something tells me, but it is not love,
I would not lose you; and you know yourself
Hate counsels not in such a quality.
But lest you should not understand me well –
And yet a maiden hath no tongue but thought –
I would detain you here some month or two
Before you venture for me. I could teach you   10
How to choose right, but then I am forsworn.
So will I never be. So may you miss me.
But if you do, you'll make me wish a sin,
That I had been forsworn. Beshrew your eyes!
They have o'erlooked me and divided me;
One half of me is yours, the other half yours,

Mine own I would say; but if mine then yours,
And so all yours. O these naughty times
Puts bars between the owners and their rights.
20   And so, though yours, not yours. Prove it so,
Let fortune go to hell for it, not I.
I speak too long, but 'tis to piece the time,
To eke it and to draw it out in length,
To stay you from election.

BASSANIO   Let me choose,
For as I am, I live upon the rack.

PORTIA
Upon the rack, Bassanio? Then confess
What treason there is mingled with your love.

BASSANIO
None but that ugly treason of mistrust
Which makes me fear th'enjoying of my love.
30   There may as well be amity and life
'Tween snow and fire, as treason and my love.

PORTIA
Ay, but I fear you speak upon the rack,
Where men enforcèd do speak anything.

BASSANIO
Promise me life and I'll confess the truth.

PORTIA
Well then, confess and live.

BASSANIO   Confess and love
Had been the very sum of my confession.
O happy torment, when my torturer
Doth teach me answers for deliverance.
But let me to my fortune and the caskets.

PORTIA
40   Away then, I am locked in one of them;
If you do love me, you will find me out.
Nerissa and the rest, stand all aloof.

Let music sound while he doth make his choice,
Then if he lose he makes a swanlike end,
Fading in music. That the comparison
May stand more proper, my eye shall be the stream
And watery deathbed for him. He may win,
And what is music then? Then music is
Even as the flourish when true subjects bow
To a new-crownèd monarch. Such it is   50
As are those dulcet sounds in break of day
That creep into the dreaming bridegroom's ear
And summon him to marriage. Now he goes,
With no less presence but with much more love
Than young Alcides when he did redeem
The virgin tribute paid by howling Troy
To the sea monster. I stand for sacrifice;
The rest aloof are the Dardanian wives,
With blearèd visages come forth to view
The issue of th'exploit. Go, Hercules;   60
Live thou, I live. With much, much more dismay
I view the fight than thou that mak'st the fray.

  A song the whilst Bassanio comments on the caskets to
  himself

    Tell me where is fancy bred,
    Or in the heart, or in the head?
    How begot, how nourishèd?
     Reply, reply.
    It is engendered in the eyes,
    With gazing fed, and fancy dies
    In the cradle where it lies.
     Let us all ring fancy's knell.   70
     I'll begin it – Ding, dong, bell.
ALL   Ding, dong, bell.
BASSANIO
So may the outward shows be least themselves.

The world is still deceived with ornament.
In law, what plea so tainted and corrupt,
But being seasoned with a gracious voice,
Obscures the show of evil? In religion,
What damnèd error but some sober brow
Will bless it and approve it with a text,
Hiding the grossness with fair ornament?
There is no vice so simple but assumes
Some mark of virtue on his outward parts.
How many cowards whose hearts are all as false
As stairs of sand, wear yet upon their chins
The beards of Hercules and frowning Mars,
Who inward searched, have livers white as milk,
And these assume but valour's excrement
To render them redoubted. Look on beauty,
And you shall see 'tis purchased by the weight,
Which therein works a miracle in nature,
Making them lightest that wear most of it.
So are those crispèd snaky golden locks,
Which make such wanton gambols with the wind
Upon supposèd fairness, often known
To be the dowry of a second head,
The skull that bred them in the sepulchre.
Thus ornament is but the guilèd shore
To a most dangerous sea, the beauteous scarf
Veiling an Indian beauty; in a word,
The seeming truth which cunning times put on
To entrap the wisest. Therefore thou gaudy gold,
Hard food for Midas, I will none of thee;
Nor none of thee, thou pale and common drudge
'Tween man and man. But thou, thou meagre lead
Which rather threaten'st than dost promise aught,
Thy paleness moves me more than eloquence,
And here choose I. Joy be the consequence!

PORTIA (*aside*)

How all the other passions fleet to air:
As doubtful thoughts, and rash-embraced despair,
And shudd'ring fear, and green-eyed jealousy.   110
O love, be moderate, allay thy ecstasy,
In measure rain thy joy, scant this excess,
I feel too much thy blessing, make it less
For fear I surfeit.

BASSANIO (*opening the leaden casket*)

              What find I here?
Fair Portia's counterfeit! What demigod
Hath come so near creation? Move these eyes?
Or whether, riding on the balls of mine,
Seem they in motion? Here are severed lips
Parted with sugar breath; so sweet a bar
Should sunder such sweet friends. Here in her hairs   120
The painter plays the spider, and hath woven
A golden mesh t'entrap the hearts of men
Faster than gnats in cobwebs. But her eyes,
How could he see to do them? Having made one,
Methinks it should have power to steal both his
And leave itself unfurnished. Yet look how far
The substance of my praise doth wrong this shadow
In underprizing it, so far this shadow
Doth limp behind the substance. Here's the scroll,
The continent and summary of my fortune: 130
    You that choose not by the view
    Chance as fair, and choose as true.
    Since this fortune falls to you,
    Be content and seek no new.
    If you be well pleased with this
    And hold your fortune for your bliss,
    Turn you where your lady is,
    And claim her with a loving kiss.

A gentle scroll. Fair lady, by your leave.
140 I come by note, to give and to receive.
Like one of two contending in a prize,
That thinks he hath done well in people's eyes,
Hearing applause and universal shout,
Giddy in spirit, still gazing in a doubt
Whether those peals of praise be his or no,
So, thrice-fair lady, stand I even so,
As doubtful whether what I see be true,
Until confirmed, signed, ratified by you.

PORTIA
You see me, Lord Bassanio, where I stand,
150 Such as I am. Though for myself alone
I would not be ambitious in my wish
To wish myself much better, yet for you
I would be trebled twenty times myself,
A thousand times more fair, ten thousand times
More rich, that only to stand high in your account,
I might in virtues, beauties, livings, friends,
Exceed account; but the full sum of me
Is sum of something, which to term in gross,
Is an unlessoned girl, unschooled, unpractisèd,
160 Happy in this, she is not yet so old
But she may learn; happier than this,
She is not bred so dull but she can learn;
Happiest of all is that her gentle spirit
Commits itself to yours to be directed,
As from her lord, her governor, her king.
Myself and what is mine to you and yours
Is now converted. But now I was the lord
Of this fair mansion, master of my servants,
Queen o'er myself; and even now, but now,
170 This house, these servants, and this same myself
Are yours, my lord's. I give them with this ring,

Which when you part from, lose, or give away,
Let it presage the ruin of your love
And be my vantage to exclaim on you.

BASSANIO

Madam, you have bereft me of all words.
Only my blood speaks to you in my veins,
And there is such confusion in my powers
As, after some oration fairly spoke
By a belovèd prince, there doth appear
Among the buzzing pleasèd multitude,   180
Where every something being blent together
Turns to a wild of nothing, save of joy
Expressed and not expressed. But when this ring
Parts from this finger, then parts life from hence,
O then be bold to say Bassanio's dead.

NERISSA

My lord and lady, it is now our time,
That have stood by and seen our wishes prosper,
To cry good joy, good joy, my lord and lady!

GRATIANO

My Lord Bassanio, and my gentle lady,
I wish you all the joy that you can wish,   190
For I am sure you can wish none from me;
And when your honours mean to solemnize
The bargain of your faith, I do beseech you
Even at that time I may be married too.

BASSANIO

With all my heart, so thou canst get a wife.

GRATIANO

I thank your lordship, you have got me one.
My eyes, my lord, can look as swift as yours:
You saw the mistress, I beheld the maid.
You loved, I loved; for intermission
No more pertains to me, my lord, than you.   200

Your fortune stood upon the caskets there,
And so did mine too, as the matter falls;
For wooing here until I sweat again,
And swearing till my very roof was dry
With oaths of love, at last, if promise last,
I got a promise of this fair one here
To have her love, provided that your fortune
Achieved her mistress.

PORTIA   Is this true, Nerissa?

NERISSA
Madam, it is, so you stand pleased withal.

BASSANIO
210 And do you, Gratiano, mean good faith?

GRATIANO
Yes, faith, my lord.

BASSANIO
Our feast shall be much honoured in your marriage.

GRATIANO We'll play with them, the first boy for a thousand ducats.

NERISSA What, and stake down?

GRATIANO No, we shall ne'er win at that sport, and stake down.
But who comes here? Lorenzo and his infidel!
What, and my old Venetian friend Salerio!

Enter Lorenzo, Jessica, and Salerio, a messenger from Venice

BASSANIO
220 Lorenzo and Salerio, welcome hither,
If that the youth of my new interest here
Have power to bid you welcome. By your leave,
I bid my very friends and countrymen,
Sweet Portia, welcome.

PORTIA   So do I, my lord.
They are entirely welcome.

LORENZO

    I thank your honour. For my part, my lord,
    My purpose was not to have seen you here,
    But meeting with Salerio by the way,
    He did entreat me past all saying nay
    To come with him along.

SALERIO   I did, my lord,   230

    And I have reason for it. Signor Antonio
    Commends him to you.

    He gives Bassanio a letter

BASSANIO   Ere I ope his letter,

    I pray you tell me how my good friend doth.

SALERIO

    Not sick, my lord, unless it be in mind,
    Nor well unless in mind. His letter there
    Will show you his estate.

    Bassanio opens the letter

GRATIANO

    Nerissa, cheer yond stranger; bid her welcome.
    Your hand, Salerio. What's the news from Venice?
    How doth that royal merchant, good Antonio?
    I know he will be glad of our success;   240
    We are the Jasons, we have won the Fleece.

SALERIO

    I would you had won the fleece that he hath lost.

PORTIA

    There are some shrewd contents in yond same paper
    That steals the colour from Bassanio's cheek:
    Some dear friend dead, else nothing in the world
    Could turn so much the constitution
    Of any constant man. What, worse and worse?
    With leave, Bassanio, I am half yourself,
    And I must freely have the half of anything
    That this same paper brings you.

250 BASSANIO   O sweet Portia,
     Here are a few of the unpleasant'st words
     That ever blotted paper! Gentle lady,
     When I did first impart my love to you,
     I freely told you all the wealth I had
     Ran in my veins – I was a gentleman –
     And then I told you true; and yet, dear lady,
     Rating myself at nothing, you shall see
     How much I was a braggart. When I told you
     My state was nothing, I should then have told you
260 That I was worse than nothing; for indeed
     I have engaged myself to a dear friend,
     Engaged my friend to his mere enemy
     To feed my means. Here is a letter, lady,
     The paper as the body of my friend,
     And every word in it a gaping wound
     Issuing life-blood. But is it true, Salerio?
     Hath all his ventures failed? What, not one hit?
     From Tripolis, from Mexico and England,
     From Lisbon, Barbary, and India,
270 And not one vessel scape the dreadful touch
     Of merchant-marring rocks?
    SALERIO   Not one, my lord.
     Besides, it should appear that if he had
     The present money to discharge the Jew,
     He would not take it. Never did I know
     A creature that did bear the shape of man
     So keen and greedy to confound a man.
     He plies the Duke at morning and at night,
     And doth impeach the freedom of the state
     If they deny him justice. Twenty merchants,
280 The Duke himself, and the magnificoes
     Of greatest port have all persuaded with him,
     But none can drive him from the envious plea

Of forfeiture, of justice, and his bond.

JESSICA

When I was with him, I have heard him swear
To Tubal and to Chus, his countrymen,
That he would rather have Antonio's flesh
Than twenty times the value of the sum
That he did owe him, and I know, my lord,
If law, authority, and power deny not,
It will go hard with poor Antonio.   290

PORTIA

Is it your dear friend that is thus in trouble?

BASSANIO

The dearest friend to me, the kindest man,
The best-conditioned and unwearied spirit
In doing courtesies, and one in whom
The ancient Roman honour more appears
Than any that draws breath in Italy.

PORTIA

What sum owes he the Jew?

BASSANIO

For me, three thousand ducats.

PORTIA   What, no more?
Pay him six thousand, and deface the bond.
Double six thousand and then treble that,   300
Before a friend of this description
Shall lose a hair through Bassanio's fault.
First go with me to church and call me wife,
And then away to Venice to your friend!
For never shall you lie by Portia's side
With an unquiet soul. You shall have gold
To pay the petty debt twenty times over.
When it is paid, bring your true friend along.
My maid Nerissa and myself meantime
Will live as maids and widows. Come away,   310

123

For you shall hence upon your wedding day.
Bid your friends welcome, show a merry cheer;
Since you are dear bought, I will love you dear.
But let me hear the letter of your friend.

BASSANIO *Sweet Bassanio, my ships have all miscarried,*
my creditors grow cruel, my estate is very low, my bond
to the Jew is forfeit. And since in paying it, it is impossible
I should live, all debts are cleared between you and I if I
might but see you at my death. Notwithstanding, use your
320 *pleasure. If your love do not persuade you to come, let not*
my letter.

PORTIA
O love, dispatch all business and be gone.

BASSANIO
Since I have your good leave to go away,
I will make haste, but till I come again
No bed shall e'er be guilty of my stay,
Nor rest be interposer 'twixt us twain.   *Exeunt*

III.3   *Enter Shylock the Jew and Solanio and Antonio and*
          the Gaoler

SHYLOCK
Gaoler, look to him. Tell not me of mercy.
This is the fool that lent out money gratis.
Gaoler, look to him.

ANTONIO   Hear me yet, good Shylock.

SHYLOCK
I'll have my bond! Speak not against my bond!
I have sworn an oath that I will have my bond.
Thou call'dst me dog before thou hadst a cause,
But since I am a dog, beware my fangs.
The Duke shall grant me justice. I do wonder,
Thou naughty gaoler, that thou art so fond

To come abroad with him at his request.   10

ANTONIO

  I pray thee hear me speak.

SHYLOCK

  I'll have my bond. I will not hear thee speak.
  I'll have my bond, and therefore speak no more.
  I'll not be made a soft and dull-eyed fool,
  To shake the head, relent, and sigh, and yield
  To Christian intercessors. Follow not.
  I'll have no speaking, I will have my bond.   *Exit*

SOLANIO

  It is the most impenetrable cur
  That ever kept with men.

ANTONIO   Let him alone.

  I'll follow him no more with bootless prayers.   20
  He seeks my life. His reason well I know:
  I oft delivered from his forfeitures
  Many that have at times made moan to me.
  Therefore he hates me.

SOLANIO   I am sure the Duke

  Will never grant this forfeiture to hold.

ANTONIO

  The Duke cannot deny the course of law,
  For the commodity that strangers have
  With us in Venice, if it be denied,
  Will much impeach the justice of the state,
  Since that the trade and profit of the city   30
  Consisteth of all nations. Therefore go.
  These griefs and losses have so bated me
  That I shall hardly spare a pound of flesh
  Tomorrow to my bloody creditor.
  Well, Gaoler, on. Pray Bassanio come
  To see me pay his debt, and then I care not.   *Exeunt*

Enter Portia, Nerissa, Lorenzo, Jessica, and Balthasar, a Man of Portia's

LORENZO

Madam, although I speak it in your presence,
You have a noble and a true conceit
Of godlike amity, which appears most strongly
In bearing thus the absence of your lord.
But if you knew to whom you show this honour,
How true a gentleman you send relief,
How dear a lover of my lord your husband,
I know you would be prouder of the work
Than customary bounty can enforce you.

PORTIA

10 I never did repent for doing good,
Nor shall not now; for in companions
That do converse and waste the time together,
Whose souls do bear an equal yoke of love,
There must be needs a like proportion
Of lineaments, of manners, and of spirit;
Which makes me think that this Antonio,
Being the bosom lover of my lord,
Must needs be like my lord. If it be so,
How little is the cost I have bestowed
20 In purchasing the semblance of my soul
From out the state of hellish cruelty.
This comes too near the praising of myself,
Therefore no more of it. Hear other things:
Lorenzo, I commit into your hands
The husbandry and manage of my house
Until my lord's return. For mine own part,
I have toward heaven breathed a secret vow
To live in prayer and contemplation,
Only attended by Nerissa here,
30 Until her husband and my lord's return.

There is a monastery two miles off,
And there we will abide. I do desire you
Not to deny this imposition,
The which my love and some necessity
Now lays upon you.

LORENZO　　　　　Madam, with all my heart,
I shall obey you in all fair commands.

PORTIA
My people do already know my mind
And will acknowledge you and Jessica
In place of Lord Bassanio and myself.
So fare you well till we shall meet again.　　　40

LORENZO
Fair thoughts and happy hours attend on you!

JESSICA
I wish your ladyship all heart's content.

PORTIA
I thank you for your wish, and am well pleased
To wish it back on you. Fare you well, Jessica.
　　　　　　　　　　Exeunt Jessica and Lorenzo
Now, Balthasar,
As I have ever found thee honest-true,
So let me find thee still. Take this same letter,
And use thou all th'endeavour of a man
In speed to Padua. See thou render this
Into my cousin's hand, Doctor Bellario,　　　50
And look what notes and garments he doth give thee
Bring them, I pray thee, with imagined speed
Unto the traject, to the common ferry
Which trades to Venice. Waste no time in words
But get thee gone. I shall be there before thee.

BALTHASAR
Madam, I go with all convenient speed.
　　　　　　　　　　　　　　　　Exit

PORTIA

Come on, Nerissa; I have work in hand
That you yet know not of. We'll see our husbands
Before they think of us.

NERISSA   Shall they see us?

PORTIA

60 They shall, Nerissa, but in such a habit
That they shall think we are accomplishèd
With that we lack. I'll hold thee any wager,
When we are both accoutered like young men,
I'll prove the prettier fellow of the two,
And wear my dagger with the braver grace,
And speak between the change of man and boy
With a reed voice, and turn two mincing steps
Into a manly stride, and speak of frays
Like a fine bragging youth, and tell quaint lies,
70 How honourable ladies sought my love,
Which I denying, they fell sick and died –
I could not do withal. Then I'll repent,
And wish, for all that, that I had not killed them.
And twenty of these puny lies I'll tell,
That men shall swear I have discontinued school
Above a twelve month. I have within my mind
A thousand raw tricks of these bragging Jacks,
Which I will practise.

NERISSA   Why, shall we turn to men?

PORTIA

Fie, what a question's that,
80 If thou wert near a lewd interpreter!
But come, I'll tell thee all my whole device
When I am in my coach, which stays for us
At the park gate, and therefore haste away,
For we must measure twenty miles today.   *Exeunt*

LAUNCELOT Yes truly, for look you, the sins of the father
are to be laid upon the children. Therefore, I promise
you I fear you. I was always plain with you, and so now
I speak my agitation of the matter. Therefore be o'good
cheer, for truly I think you are damned. There is but
one hope in it that can do you any good, and that is but a
kind of bastard hope neither.

JESSICA And what hope is that, I pray thee?

LAUNCELOT Marry, you may partly hope that your father
got you not, that you are not the Jew's daughter.   10

JESSICA That were a kind of bastard hope indeed! So the
sins of my mother should be visited upon me.

LAUNCELOT Truly then, I fear you are damned both by
father and mother. Thus when I shun Scylla your father,
I fall into Charybdis your mother. Well, you are gone
both ways.

JESSICA I shall be saved by my husband. He hath made
me a Christian.

LAUNCELOT Truly, the more to blame he! We were
Christians enow before, e'en as many as could well live 20
one by another. This making of Christians will raise the
price of hogs; if we grow all to be pork-eaters, we shall
not shortly have a rasher on the coals for money.

    Enter Lorenzo

JESSICA I'll tell my husband, Launcelot, what you say.
Here he comes.

LORENZO I shall grow jealous of you shortly, Launcelot,
if you thus get my wife into corners.

JESSICA Nay, you need not fear us, Lorenzo. Launcelot
and I are out. He tells me flatly there's no mercy for me
in heaven because I am a Jew's daughter, and he says you 30
are no good member of the commonwealth, for in converting Jews to Christians you raise the price of pork.

LORENZO (*to Launcelot*) I shall answer that better to the commonwealth than you can the getting up of the Negro's belly. The Moor is with child by you, Launcelot.

LAUNCELOT It is much that the Moor should be more than reason; but if she be less than an honest woman, she is indeed more than I took her for.

40 LORENZO How every fool can play upon the word! I think the best grace of wit will shortly turn into silence, and discourse grow commendable in none only but parrots. Go in, sirrah, bid them prepare for dinner.

LAUNCELOT That is done, sir. They have all stomachs.

LORENZO Goodly Lord, what a wit-snapper are you! Then bid them prepare dinner.

LAUNCELOT That is done too, sir. Only 'cover' is the word.

LORENZO Will you cover then, sir?

50 LAUNCELOT Not so, sir, neither. I know my duty.

LORENZO Yet more quarrelling with occasion. Wilt thou show the whole wealth of thy wit in an instant? I pray thee understand a plain man in his plain meaning: go to thy fellows, bid them cover the table, serve in the meat, and we will come in to dinner.

LAUNCELOT For the table, sir, it shall be served in; for the meat, sir, it shall be covered; for your coming in to dinner, sir, why let it be as humours and conceits shall govern. *Exit Launcelot*

LORENZO

60   O dear discretion, how his words are suited!
    The fool hath planted in his memory
    An army of good words; and I do know
    A many fools that stand in better place,
    Garnished like him, that for a tricksy word
    Defy the matter. How cheer'st thou, Jessica?

And now, good sweet, say thy opinion,
How dost thou like the Lord Bassanio's wife?

JESSICA
Past all expressing. It is very meet
The Lord Bassanio live an upright life,
For having such a blessing in his lady,   70
He finds the joys of heaven here on earth,
And if on earth he do not merit it,
In reason he should never come to heaven.
Why, if two gods should play some heavenly match
And on the wager lay two earthly women,
And Portia one, there must be something else
Pawned with the other, for the poor rude world
Hath not her fellow.

LORENZO   Even such a husband
Hast thou of me as she is for a wife.

JESSICA
Nay, but ask my opinion too of that!   80

LORENZO
I will anon. First let us go to dinner.

JESSICA
Nay, let me praise you while I have a stomach.

LORENZO
No, pray thee, let it serve for table-talk,
Then howsome'er thou speak'st, 'mong other things
I shall digest it.

JESSICA   Well, I'll set you forth.   *Exeunt*

✳

Enter the Duke, the magnificoes, Antonio, Bassanio,   IV.1
Salerio, and Gratiano with others

DUKE
What, is Antonio here?

131

ANTONIO

Ready, so please your grace.

DUKE

I am sorry for thee. Thou art come to answer
A stony adversary, an inhuman wretch,
Uncapable of pity, void and empty
From any dram of mercy.

ANTONIO   I have heard
Your grace hath ta'en great pains to qualify
His rigorous course; but since he stands obdurate,
And that no lawful means can carry me
10 Out of his envy's reach, I do oppose
My patience to his fury, and am armed
To suffer with a quietness of spirit
The very tyranny and rage of his.

DUKE

Go one, and call the Jew into the court.

SALERIO

He is ready at the door; he comes, my lord.
        Enter Shylock

DUKE

Make room, and let him stand before our face.
Shylock, the world thinks, and I think so too,
That thou but lead'st this fashion of thy malice
To the last hour of act, and then 'tis thought
20 Thou'lt show thy mercy and remorse more strange
Than is thy strange apparent cruelty;
And where thou now exacts the penalty,
Which is a pound of this poor merchant's flesh,
Thou wilt not only loose the forfeiture,
But touched with human gentleness and love,
Forgive a moiety of the principal,
Glancing an eye of pity on his losses,
That have of late so huddled on his back,

Enow to press a royal merchant down
And pluck commiseration of his state   30
From brassy bosoms and rough hearts of flint,
From stubborn Turks and Tartars never trained
To offices of tender courtesy.
We all expect a gentle answer, Jew.

SHYLOCK

I have possessed your grace of what I purpose,
And by our holy Sabbath have I sworn
To have the due and forfeit of my bond.
If you deny it, let the danger light
Upon your charter and your city's freedom!
You'll ask me why I rather choose to have   40
A weight of carrion flesh than to receive
Three thousand ducats. I'll not answer that,
But say it is my humour. Is it answered?
What if my house be troubled with a rat,
And I be pleased to give ten thousand ducats
To have it baned? What, are you answered yet?
Some men there are love not a gaping pig,
Some that are mad if they behold a cat,
And others, when the bagpipe sings i'th'nose,
Cannot contain their urine; for affection,   50
Master of passion, sways it to the mood
Of what it likes or loathes. Now for your answer:
As there is no firm reason to be rendered
Why he cannot abide a gaping pig,
Why he a harmless necessary cat,
Why he a woollen bagpipe, but of force
Must yield to such inevitable shame
As to offend, himself being offended;
So can I give no reason, nor I will not,
More than a lodged hate and a certain loathing   60
I bear Antonio, that I follow thus

A losing suit against him. Are you answered?

BASSANIO

This is no answer, thou unfeeling man,
To excuse the current of thy cruelty.

SHYLOCK

I am not bound to please thee with my answers.

BASSANIO

Do all men kill the things they do not love?

SHYLOCK

Hates any man the thing he would not kill?

BASSANIO

Every offence is not a hate at first.

SHYLOCK

What, wouldst thou have a serpent sting thee twice?

ANTONIO

70 I pray you think you question with the Jew.
You may as well go stand upon the beach
And bid the main flood bate his usual height,
You may as well use question with the wolf
Why he hath made the ewe bleat for the lamb,
You may as well forbid the mountain pines
To wag their high-tops and to make no noise
When they are fretten with the gusts of heaven;
You may as well do anything most hard
As seek to soften that – than which what's harder? –
80 His Jewish heart. Therefore I do beseech you
Make no more offers, use no farther means,
But with all brief and plain conveniency
Let me have judgement, and the Jew his will.

BASSANIO

For thy three thousand ducats here is six.

SHYLOCK

If every ducat in six thousand ducats
Were in six parts, and every part a ducat,

I would not draw them. I would have my bond.

DUKE

How shalt thou hope for mercy, rendering none?

SHYLOCK

What judgement shall I dread, doing no wrong?
You have among you many a purchased slave,   90
Which like your asses and your dogs and mules
You use in abject and in slavish parts,
Because you bought them. Shall I say to you,
'Let them be free! Marry them to your heirs!
Why sweat they under burdens? Let their beds
Be made as soft as yours, and let their palates
Be seasoned with such viands'? You will answer,
'The slaves are ours.' So do I answer you.
The pound of flesh which I demand of him
Is dearly bought, 'tis mine, and I will have it.   100
If you deny me, fie upon your law!
There is no force in the decrees of Venice.
I stand for judgement. Answer; shall I have it?

DUKE

Upon my power I may dismiss this court
Unless Bellario, a learned doctor
Whom I have sent for to determine this,
Come here today.

SALERIO   My lord, here stays without
A messenger with letters from the doctor,
New come from Padua.

DUKE

Bring us the letters. Call the messenger.   110

BASSANIO

Good cheer, Antonio! What, man, courage yet!
The Jew shall have my flesh, blood, bones, and all,
Ere thou shalt lose for me one drop of blood.

ANTONIO

    I am a tainted wether of the flock,
    Meetest for death. The weakest kind of fruit
    Drops earliest to the ground, and so let me.
    You cannot better be employed, Bassanio,
    Than to live still, and write mine epitaph.
        Enter Nerissa dressed like a lawyer's clerk

DUKE

    Came you from Padua, from Bellario?

NERISSA

120   From both, my lord. Bellario greets your grace.
        She presents a letter

BASSANIO

    Why dost thou whet thy knife so earnestly?

SHYLOCK

    To cut the forfeiture from that bankrupt there.

GRATIANO

    Not on thy sole, but on thy soul, harsh Jew,
    Thou mak'st thy knife keen; but no metal can,
    No, not the hangman's axe, bear half the keenness
    Of thy sharp envy. Can no prayers pierce thee?

SHYLOCK

    No, none that thou hast wit enough to make.

GRATIANO

    O be thou damned, inexecrable dog,
    And for thy life let justice be accused!
130   Thou almost mak'st me waver in my faith,
    To hold opinion with Pythagoras
    That souls of animals infuse themselves
    Into the trunks of men. Thy currish spirit
    Governed a wolf who, hanged for human slaughter,
    Even from the gallows did his fell soul fleet,
    And whilst thou layest in thy unhallowed dam,
    Infused itself in thee; for thy desires

Are wolvish, bloody, starved, and ravenous.

SHYLOCK

Till thou canst rail the seal from off my bond,
Thou but offend'st thy lungs to speak so loud.　　140
Repair thy wit, good youth, or it will fall
To cureless ruin. I stand here for law.

DUKE

This letter from Bellario doth commend
A young and learned doctor to our court.
Where is he?

NERISSA　　　　He attendeth here hard by
To know your answer whether you'll admit him.

DUKE

With all my heart. Some three or four of you
Go give him courteous conduct to this place.
Meantime the court shall hear Bellario's letter.

CLERK *Your grace shall understand that at the receipt of* 150
your letter I am very sick; but in the instant that your
messenger came, in loving visitation was with me a young
doctor of Rome. His name is Balthasar. I acquainted
him with the cause in controversy between the Jew and
Antonio the merchant. We turned o'er many books to-
gether. He is furnished with my opinion which, bettered
with his own learning, the greatness whereof I cannot
enough commend, comes with him at my importunity to fill
up your grace's request in my stead. I beseech you let his
lack of years be no impediment to let him lack a reverend 160
estimation, for I never knew so young a body with so old a
head. I leave him to your gracious acceptance, whose trial
shall better publish his commendation.

Enter Portia as Balthasar, dressed like a Doctor of Laws

DUKE

You hear the learn'd Bellario, what he writes,

And here, I take it, is the doctor come.
Give me your hand. Came you from old Bellario?

PORTIA
I did, my lord.

DUKE   You are welcome; take your place.
Are you acquainted with the difference
That holds this present question in the court?

PORTIA
170 I am informèd throughly of the cause.
Which is the merchant here? And which the Jew?

DUKE
Antonio and old Shylock, both stand forth.

PORTIA
Is your name Shylock?

SHYLOCK   Shylock is my name.

PORTIA
Of a strange nature is the suit you follow,
Yet in such rule that the Venetian law
Cannot impugn you as you do proceed.
(to Antonio) You stand within his danger, do you not?

ANTONIO
Ay, so he says.

PORTIA   Do you confess the bond?

ANTONIO
I do.

PORTIA   Then must the Jew be merciful.

SHYLOCK
180 On what compulsion must I? Tell me that.

PORTIA
The quality of mercy is not strained,
It droppeth as the gentle rain from heaven
Upon the place beneath. It is twice blest,
It blesseth him that gives and him that takes.
'Tis mightiest in the mightiest, it becomes
The thronèd monarch better than his crown.

138

His sceptre shows the force of temporal power,
The attribute to awe and majesty,
Wherein doth sit the dread and fear of kings;
But mercy is above this sceptred sway,   190
It is enthronèd in the hearts of kings,
It is an attribute to God himself,
And earthly power doth then show likest God's
When mercy seasons justice. Therefore, Jew,
Though justice be thy plea, consider this:
That in the course of justice none of us
Should see salvation. We do pray for mercy,
And that same prayer doth teach us all to render
The deeds of mercy. I have spoke thus much
To mitigate the justice of thy plea,   200
Which if thou follow, this strict court of Venice
Must needs give sentence 'gainst the merchant there.

SHYLOCK

My deeds upon my head! I crave the law,
The penalty and forfeit of my bond.

PORTIA

Is he not able to discharge the money?

BASSANIO

Yes, here I tender it for him in the court,
Yea, twice the sum. If that will not suffice,
I will be bound to pay it ten times o'er
On forfeit of my hands, my head, my heart.
If this will not suffice, it must appear   210
That malice bears down truth. And I beseech you,
Wrest once the law to your authority,
To do a great right, do a little wrong,
And curb this cruel devil of his will.

PORTIA

It must not be. There is no power in Venice
Can alter a decree establishèd.
'Twill be recorded for a precedent,

And many an error by the same example
Will rush into the state. It cannot be.

SHYLOCK

220   A Daniel come to judgement! Yea, a Daniel!
O wise young judge, how I do honour thee!

PORTIA

I pray you let me look upon the bond.

SHYLOCK

Here 'tis, most reverend doctor, here it is.

PORTIA

Shylock, there's thrice thy money offered thee.

SHYLOCK

An oath, an oath! I have an oath in heaven;
Shall I lay perjury upon my soul?
No, not for Venice!

PORTIA   Why, this bond is forfeit,
And lawfully by this the Jew may claim
A pound of flesh, to be by him cut off

230   Nearest the merchant's heart. Be merciful,
Take thrice thy money, bid me tear the bond.

SHYLOCK

When it is paid, according to the tenour.
It doth appear you are a worthy judge,
You know the law, your exposition
Hath been most sound. I charge you by the law,
Whereof you are a well-deserving pillar,
Proceed to judgement. By my soul I swear
There is no power in the tongue of man
To alter me. I stay here on my bond.

ANTONIO

240   Most heartily I do beseech the court
To give the judgement.

PORTIA   Why then, thus it is:

You must prepare your bosom for his knife.

SHYLOCK

O noble judge! O excellent young man!

PORTIA

For the intent and purpose of the law
Hath full relation to the penalty,
Which here appeareth due upon the bond.

SHYLOCK

'Tis very true. O wise and upright judge!
How much more elder art thou than thy looks!

PORTIA

Therefore lay bare your bosom.

SHYLOCK   Ay, his breast,
So says the bond, doth it not, noble judge?   250
'Nearest his heart', those are the very words.

PORTIA

It is so. Are there balance here to weigh
The flesh?

SHYLOCK   I have them ready.

PORTIA

Have by some surgeon, Shylock, on your charge,
To stop his wounds, lest he do bleed to death.

SHYLOCK

Is it so nominated in the bond?

PORTIA

It is not so expressed, but what of that?
'Twere good you do so much for charity.

SHYLOCK

I cannot find it; 'tis not in the bond.

PORTIA

You, merchant, have you anything to say?   260

ANTONIO

But little. I am armed and well prepared.
Give me your hand, Bassanio, fare you well.

Grieve not that I am fallen to this for you,
For herein Fortune shows herself more kind
Than is her custom; it is still her use
To let the wretched man outlive his wealth
To view with hollow eye and wrinkled brow
An age of poverty, from which lingering penance
Of such misery doth she cut me off.

270   Commend me to your honourable wife,
Tell her the process of Antonio's end,
Say how I loved you, speak me fair in death,
And when the tale is told, bid her be judge
Whether Bassanio had not once a love.
Repent but you that you shall lose your friend,
And he repents not that he pays your debt,
For if the Jew do cut but deep enough,
I'll pay it instantly with all my heart.

BASSANIO

Antonio, I am married to a wife
280   Which is as dear to me as life itself,
But life itself, my wife, and all the world
Are not with me esteemed above thy life.
I would lose all, ay sacrifice them all
Here to this devil, to deliver you.

PORTIA

Your wife would give you little thanks for that
If she were by to hear you make the offer.

GRATIANO

I have a wife who I protest I love;
I would she were in heaven, so she could
Entreat some power to change this currish Jew.

NERISSA

290   'Tis well you offer it behind her back,
The wish would make else an unquiet house.

SHYLOCK

These be the Christian husbands! I have a daughter;

Would any of the stock of Barabbas
Had been her husband, rather than a Christian.
We trifle time. I pray thee pursue sentence.

PORTIA
A pound of that same merchant's flesh is thine,
The court awards it, and the law doth give it.

SHYLOCK
Most rightful judge!

PORTIA
And you must cut this flesh from off his breast,
The law allows it, and the court awards it.   300

SHYLOCK
Most learned judge! A sentence! Come, prepare!

PORTIA
Tarry a little, there is something else.
This bond doth give thee here no jot of blood;
The words expressly are 'a pound of flesh'.
Take then thy bond, take thou thy pound of flesh,
But in the cutting it if thou dost shed
One drop of Christian blood, thy lands and goods
Are by the laws of Venice confiscate
Unto the state of Venice.

GRATIANO
O upright judge! Mark, Jew. O learned judge!   310

SHYLOCK
Is that the law?

PORTIA   Thyself shalt see the act,
For, as thou urgest justice, be assured
Thou shalt have justice more than thou desir'st.

GRATIANO
O learned judge! Mark, Jew. A learned judge!

SHYLOCK
I take this offer then. Pay the bond thrice
And let the Christian go.

BASSANIO   Here is the money.

PORTIA

Soft!

The Jew shall have all justice. Soft, no haste,

He shall have nothing but the penalty.

GRATIANO

320   O Jew! An upright judge, a learned judge!

PORTIA

Therefore prepare thee to cut off the flesh.

Shed thou no blood, nor cut thou less nor more

But just a pound of flesh. If thou tak'st more

Or less than a just pound, be it but so much

As makes it light or heavy in the substance

Or the division of the twentieth part

Of one poor scruple, nay, if the scale do turn

But in the estimation of a hair,

Thou diest, and all thy goods are confiscate.

GRATIANO

330   A second Daniel! A Daniel, Jew!

Now, infidel, I have you on the hip!

PORTIA

Why doth the Jew pause? Take thy forfeiture.

SHYLOCK

Give me my principal, and let me go.

BASSANIO

I have it ready for thee; here it is.

PORTIA

He hath refused it in the open court.

He shall have merely justice and his bond.

GRATIANO

A Daniel still say I, a second Daniel!

I thank thee, Jew, for teaching me that word.

SHYLOCK

Shall I not have barely my principal?

PORTIA

    Thou shalt have nothing but the forfeiture,   340
    To be so taken at thy peril, Jew.

SHYLOCK

    Why, then the devil give him good of it!
    I'll stay no longer question.

PORTIA   Tarry, Jew!
    The law hath yet another hold on you.
    It is enacted in the laws of Venice,
    If it be proved against an alien
    That by direct or indirect attempts
    He seek the life of any citizen,
    The party 'gainst the which he doth contrive
    Shall seize one half his goods, the other half   350
    Comes to the privy coffer of the state,
    And the offender's life lies in the mercy
    Of the Duke only, 'gainst all other voice,
    In which predicament I say thou stand'st,
    For it appears by manifest proceeding
    That indirectly, and directly too,
    Thou hast contrived against the very life
    Of the defendant, and thou hast incurred
    The danger formerly by me rehearsed.
    Down therefore, and beg mercy of the Duke.   360

GRATIANO

    Beg that thou mayst have leave to hang thyself,
    And yet, thy wealth being forfeit to the state,
    Thou hast not left the value of a cord,
    Therefore thou must be hanged at the state's charge.

DUKE

    That thou shalt see the difference of our spirit,
    I pardon thee thy life before thou ask it.
    For half thy wealth, it is Antonio's,
    The other half comes to the general state,

Which humbleness may drive unto a fine.

PORTIA

370   Ay, for the state, not for Antonio.

SHYLOCK

Nay, take my life and all! Pardon not that!
You take my house when you do take the prop
That doth sustain my house. You take my life
When you do take the means whereby I live.

PORTIA

What mercy can you render him, Antonio?

GRATIANO.

A halter gratis! Nothing else, for God's sake!

ANTONIO

So please my lord the Duke and all the court
To quit the fine for one half of his goods,
I am content, so he will let me have

380   The other half in use, to render it
Upon his death unto the gentleman
That lately stole his daughter.
Two things provided more: that for this favour
He presently become a Christian;
The other, that he do record a gift
Here in the court of all he dies possessed
Unto his son Lorenzo and his daughter.

DUKE

He shall do this, or else I do recant
The pardon that I late pronouncèd here.

PORTIA

390   Art thou contented, Jew? What dost thou say?

SHYLOCK

I am content.

PORTIA   Clerk, draw a deed of gift.

SHYLOCK

I pray you give me leave to go from hence,

I am not well; send the deed after me,
And I will sign it.

DUKE   Get thee gone, but do it.

GRATIANO

In christ'ning shalt thou have two godfathers.
Had I been judge, thou shouldst have had ten more,
To bring thee to the gallows, not to the font.

Exit Shylock

DUKE

Sir, I entreat you home with me to dinner.

PORTIA

I humbly do desire your grace of pardon.
I must away this night toward Padua,   400
And it is meet I presently set forth.

DUKE

I am sorry that your leisure serves you not.
Antonio, gratify this gentleman,
For in my mind you are much bound to him.

Exit Duke and his train

BASSANIO

Most worthy gentleman, I and my friend
Have by your wisdom been this day acquitted
Of grievous penalties, in lieu whereof
Three thousand ducats due unto the Jew
We freely cope your courteous pains withal.

ANTONIO

And stand indebted, over and above,   410
In love and service to you evermore.

PORTIA

He is well paid that is well satisfied,
And I delivering you am satisfied,
And therein do account myself well paid;
My mind was never yet more mercenary.
I pray you know me when we meet again,

I wish you well, and so I take my leave.

BASSANIO

Dear sir, of force I must attempt you further.

Take some remembrance of us as a tribute,

420 Not as fee. Grant me two things, I pray you:

Not to deny me, and to pardon me.

PORTIA

You press me far, and therefore I will yield.

Give me your gloves, I'll wear them for your sake.

Bassanio takes off his gloves

And for your love I'll take this ring from you.

Do not draw back your hand, I'll take no more,

And you in love shall not deny me this.

BASSANIO

This ring, good sir, alas, it is a trifle!

I will not shame myself to give you this.

PORTIA

I will have nothing else but only this,

430 And now methinks I have a mind to it.

BASSANIO

There's more depends on this than on the value.

The dearest ring in Venice will I give you,

And find it out by proclamation.

Only for this, I pray you pardon me.

PORTIA

I see, sir, you are liberal in offers.

You taught me first to beg, and now methinks

You teach me how a beggar should be answered.

BASSANIO

Good sir, this ring was given me by my wife,

And when she put it on she made me vow

440 That I should neither sell nor give nor lose it.

PORTIA

That 'scuse serves many men to save their gifts,

And if your wife be not a madwoman,
And know how well I have deserved this ring,
She would not hold out enemy for ever
For giving it to me. Well, peace be with you!

Exeunt Portia and Nerissa

ANTONIO
My Lord Bassanio, let him have the ring.
Let his deservings, and my love withal,
Be valued 'gainst your wife's commandèment.

BASSANIO
Go, Gratiano, run and overtake him,
Give him the ring and bring him if thou canst   450
Unto Antonio's house. Away, make haste!

Exit Gratiano

Come, you and I will thither presently,
And in the morning early will we both
Fly toward Belmont. Come, Antonio.   *Exeunt*

Enter Portia and Nerissa, disguised as before   IV.2

PORTIA
Inquire the Jew's house out, give him this deed,
And let him sign it. We'll away tonight
And be a day before our husbands home.
This deed will be well welcome to Lorenzo.
Enter Gratiano

GRATIANO
Fair sir, you are well o'erta'en.
My Lord Bassanio upon more advice
Hath sent you here this ring, and doth entreat
Your company at dinner.

PORTIA   That cannot be.
His ring I do accept most thankfully,
And so I pray you tell him. Furthermore,   10

I pray you show my youth old Shylock's house.
GRATIANO
That will I do.
NERISSA   Sir, I would speak with you.
   (*aside to Portia*) I'll see if I can get my husband's ring,
Which I did make him swear to keep for ever.
PORTIA (*aside to Nerissa*)
Thou mayst, I warrant. We shall have old swearing
That they did give the rings away to men,
But we'll outface them, and outswear them too.
Away, make haste. Thou know'st where I will tarry.
NERISSA
Come, good sir, will you show me to this house?

Exeunt

*

V.1   *Enter Lorenzo and Jessica*
LORENZO
   The moon shines bright. In such a night as this,
   When the sweet wind did gently kiss the trees
   And they did make no noise, in such a night
   Troilus methinks mounted the Troyan walls,
   And sighed his soul toward the Grecian tents
   Where Cressid lay that night.
JESSICA   In such a night
   Did Thisbe fearfully o'ertrip the dew,
   And saw the lion's shadow ere himself,
   And ran dismayed away.
LORENZO   In such a night
10 Stood Dido with a willow in her hand
   Upon the wild sea banks, and waft her love
   To come again to Carthage.

JESSICA   In such a night
Medea gathered the enchanted herbs
That did renew old Aeson.

LORENZO   In such a night
Did Jessica steal from the wealthy Jew,
And with an unthrift love did run from Venice
As far as Belmont.

JESSICA   In such a night
Did young Lorenzo swear he loved her well,
Stealing her soul with many vows of faith,
And ne'er a true one.

LORENZO   In such a night   20
Did pretty Jessica, like a little shrew,
Slander her love, and he forgave it her.

JESSICA
I would out-night you, did nobody come;
But hark, I hear the footing of a man.
        Enter Stephano

LORENZO
Who comes so fast in silence of the night?

STEPHANO
A friend.

LORENZO
A friend? What friend? Your name I pray you, friend.

STEPHANO
Stephano is my name, and I bring word
My mistress will before the break of day
Be here at Belmont. She doth stray about   30
By holy crosses where she kneels and prays
For happy wedlock hours.

LORENZO   Who comes with her?

STEPHANO
None but a holy hermit and her maid.
I pray you, is my master yet returned?

LORENZO

He is not, nor we have not heard from him.
But go we in, I pray thee, Jessica,
And ceremoniously let us prepare
Some welcome for the mistress of the house.

Enter Launcelot

LAUNCELOT Sola, sola! Wo ha ho! Sola, sola!

40 **LORENZO** Who calls?

LAUNCELOT Sola! Did you see Master Lorenzo? Master
Lorenzo! Sola, sola!

LORENZO Leave holloaing, man! Here.

LAUNCELOT Sola! Where? Where?

LORENZO Here!

LAUNCELOT Tell him there's a post come from my
master, with his horn full of good news. My master will
be here ere morning.   *Exit*

LORENZO

Sweet soul, let's in, and there expect their coming.
50 And yet no matter, why should we go in?
My friend Stephano, signify, I pray you,
Within the house, your mistress is at hand,
And bring your music forth into the air.   *Exit Stephano*
How sweet the moonlight sleeps upon this bank!
Here will we sit and let the sounds of music
Creep in our ears; soft stillness and the night
Become the touches of sweet harmony.
Sit, Jessica. Look how the floor of heaven
Is thick inlaid with patens of bright gold.
60 There's not the smallest orb which thou beholdest
But in his motion like an angel sings,
Still quiring to the young-eyed cherubins;
Such harmony is in immortal souls,
But whilst this muddy vesture of decay
Doth grossly close it in, we cannot hear it.

Enter Musicians

Come ho, and wake Diana with a hymn,
With sweetest touches pierce your mistress' ear
And draw her home with music.

Music

JESSICA

I am never merry when I hear sweet music.

LORENZO

The reason is your spirits are attentive.   70
For do but note a wild and wanton herd
Or race of youthful and unhandled colts
Fetching mad bounds, bellowing and neighing loud,
Which is the hot condition of their blood,
If they but hear perchance a trumpet sound,
Or any air of music touch their ears,
You shall perceive them make a mutual stand,
Their savage eyes turned to a modest gaze
By the sweet power of music. Therefore the poet
Did feign that Orpheus drew trees, stones, and floods,   80
Since naught so stockish, hard, and full of rage
But music for the time doth change his nature.
The man that hath no music in himself,
Nor is not moved with concord of sweet sounds,
Is fit for treasons, stratagems, and spoils,
The motions of his spirit are dull as night,
And his affections dark as Erebus.
Let no such man be trusted. Mark the music.

Enter Portia and Nerissa

PORTIA

That light we see is burning in my hall;
How far that little candle throws his beams!   90
So shines a good deed in a naughty world.

NERISSA

When the moon shone we did not see the candle.

PORTIA

So doth the greater glory dim the less.
A substitute shines brightly as a king
Until a king be by, and then his state
Empties itself, as doth an inland brook
Into the main of waters. Music! hark!

NERISSA

It is your music, madam, of the house.

PORTIA

Nothing is good, I see, without respect;
100   Methinks it sounds much sweeter than by day.

NERISSA

Silence bestows that virtue on it, madam.

PORTIA

The crow doth sing as sweetly as the lark
When neither is attended, and I think
The nightingale, if she should sing by day
When every goose is cackling, would be thought
No better a musician than the wren.
How many things by season seasoned are
To their right praise and true perfection!
Peace!

Music ceases

How the moon sleeps with Endymion,
110   And would not be awaked.

LORENZO   That is the voice,
Or I am much deceived, of Portia.

PORTIA

He knows me as the blind man knows the cuckoo,
By the bad voice.

LORENZO   Dear lady, welcome home.

PORTIA

We have been praying for our husbands' welfare,
Which speed we hope the better for our words.

Are they returned?

LORENZO   Madam, they are not yet,
But there is come a messenger before
To signify their coming.

PORTIA   Go in, Nerissa,
Give order to my servants that they take
No note at all of our being absent hence,   120
Nor you, Lorenzo, Jessica, nor you.
        A tucket sounds

LORENZO
Your husband is at hand, I hear his trumpet.
We are no tell-tales, madam; fear you not.

PORTIA
This night methinks is but the daylight sick,
It looks a little paler. 'Tis a day
Such as the day is when the sun is hid.
        Enter Bassanio, Antonio, Gratiano, and their followers

BASSANIO
We should hold day with the Antipodes
If you would walk in absence of the sun.

PORTIA
Let me give light, but let me not be light,
For a light wife doth make a heavy husband,   130
And never be Bassanio so for me.
But God sort all! You are welcome home, my lord.

BASSANIO
I thank you, madam. Give welcome to my friend.
This is the man, this is Antonio,
To whom I am so infinitely bound.

PORTIA
You should in all sense be much bound to him,
For, as I hear, he was much bound for you.

ANTONIO
No more than I am well acquitted of.

155

PORTIA

Sir, you are very welcome to our house;
140 It must appear in other ways than words,
Therefore I scant this breathing courtesy.

GRATIANO (*to Nerissa*)

By yonder moon I swear you do me wrong!
In faith, I gave it to the judge's clerk.
Would he were gelt that had it for my part
Since you do take it, love, so much at heart.

PORTIA

A quarrel ho, already! What's the matter?

GRATIANO

About a hoop of gold, a paltry ring
That she did give me, whose posy was
For all the world like cutler's poetry
150 Upon a knife, 'Love me, and leave me not.'

NERISSA

What talk you of the posy or the value?
You swore to me when I did give it you
That you would wear it till your hour of death,
And that it should lie with you in your grave.
Though not for me, yet for your vehement oaths,
You should have been respective and have kept it.
Gave it a judge's clerk! No, God's my judge,
The clerk will ne'er wear hair on's face that had it!

GRATIANO

He will, an if he live to be a man.

NERISSA

160 Ay, if a woman live to be a man.

GRATIANO

Now by this hand, I gave it to a youth,
A kind of boy, a little scrubbèd boy
No higher than thyself, the judge's clerk,
A prating boy that begged it as a fee;

I could not for my heart deny it him.

PORTIA

You were to blame – I must be plain with you –
To part so slightly with your wife's first gift,
A thing stuck on with oaths upon your finger
And so riveted with faith unto your flesh.
I gave my love a ring, and made him swear   170
Never to part with it; and here he stands.
I dare be sworn for him he would not leave it
Nor pluck it from his finger for the wealth
That the world masters. Now in faith, Gratiano,
You give your wife too unkind a cause of grief.
An 'twere to me, I should be mad at it.

BASSANIO (aside)

Why, I were best to cut my left hand off
And swear I lost the ring defending it.

GRATIANO

My Lord Bassanio gave his ring away
Unto the judge that begged it, and indeed   180
Deserved it too; and then the boy, his clerk
That took some pains in writing, he begged mine,
And neither man nor master would take aught
But the two rings.

PORTIA   What ring gave you, my lord?
Not that, I hope, which you received of me?

BASSANIO

If I could add a lie unto a fault,
I would deny it, but you see my finger
Hath not the ring upon it, it is gone.

PORTIA

Even so void is your false heart of truth.
By heaven, I will ne'er come in your bed   190
Until I see the ring!

NERISSA   Nor I in yours

    Till I again see mine!

BASSANIO   Sweet Portia,
    If you did know to whom I gave the ring,
    If you did know for whom I gave the ring,
    And would conceive for what I gave the ring,
    And how unwillingly I left the ring
    When naught would be accepted but the ring,
    You would abate the strength of your displeasure.

PORTIA
    If you had known the virtue of the ring,
200   Or half her worthiness that gave the ring,
    Or your own honour to contain the ring,
    You would not then have parted with the ring.
    What man is there so much unreasonable,
    If you had pleased to have defended it
    With any terms of zeal, wanted the modesty
    To urge the thing held as a ceremony?
    Nerissa teaches me what to believe,
    I'll die for't but some woman had the ring!

BASSANIO
    No, by my honour, madam! By my soul
210   No woman had it, but a civil doctor,
    Which did refuse three thousand ducats of me
    And begged the ring, the which I did deny him,
    And suffered him to go displeased away,
    Even he that had held up the very life
    Of my dear friend. What should I say, sweet lady?
    I was enforced to send it after him.
    I was beset with shame and courtesy.
    My honour would not let ingratitude
    So much besmear it. Pardon me, good lady!
220   For by these blessèd candles of the night,
    Had you been there I think you would have begged
    The ring of me to give the worthy doctor.

PORTIA

 Let not that doctor e'er come near my house.
 Since he hath got the jewel that I loved,
 And that which you did swear to keep for me,
 I will become as liberal as you,
 I'll not deny him anything I have,
 No, not my body nor my husband's bed.
 Know him I shall, I am well sure of it.
 Lie not a night from home; watch me like Argus.   230
 If you do not, if I be left alone,
 Now by mine honour which is yet mine own,
 I'll have that doctor for my bedfellow.

NERISSA

 And I his clerk. Therefore be well advised
 How you do leave me to mine own protection.

GRATIANO

 Well, do you so. Let not me take him then!
 For if I do, I'll mar the young clerk's pen.

ANTONIO

 I am th'unhappy subject of these quarrels.

PORTIA

 Sir, grieve not you, you are welcome notwithstanding.

BASSANIO

 Portia, forgive me this enforcèd wrong,   240
 And in the hearing of these many friends
 I swear to thee, even by thine own fair eyes,
 Wherein I see myself . . .

PORTIA   Mark you but that!
 In both my eyes he doubly sees himself,
 In each eye one. Swear by your double self,
 And there's an oath of credit.

BASSANIO   Nay, but hear me.
 Pardon this fault, and by my soul I swear
 I never more will break an oath with thee.

ANTONIO

    I once did lend my body for his wealth,

250   Which but for him that had your husband's ring

    Had quite miscarried. I dare be bound again,

    My soul upon the forfeit, that your lord

    Will never more break faith advisedly.

PORTIA

    Then you shall be his surety. Give him this,

    And bid him keep it better than the other.

ANTONIO

    Here, Lord Bassanio. Swear to keep this ring.

BASSANIO

    By heaven, it is the same I gave the doctor!

PORTIA

    I had it of him. Pardon me, Bassanio,

    For by this ring the doctor lay with me.

NERISSA

260   And pardon me, my gentle Gratiano,

    For that same scrubbèd boy, the doctor's clerk,

    In lieu of this last night did lie with me.

GRATIANO

    Why, this is like the mending of highways

    In summer, where the ways are fair enough.

    What, are we cuckolds ere we have deserved it?

PORTIA

    Speak not so grossly. You are all amazed.

    Here is a letter, read it at your leisure.

    It comes from Padua from Bellario.

    There you shall find that Portia was the doctor,

270   Nerissa there her clerk. Lorenzo here

    Shall witness I set forth as soon as you,

    And even but now returned, I have not yet

    Entered my house. Antonio, you are welcome,

    And I have better news in store for you

Than you expect. Unseal this letter soon,
There you shall find three of your argosies
Are richly come to harbour suddenly.
You shall not know by what strange accident
I chancèd on this letter.

ANTONIO   I am dumb!

BASSANIO
Were you the doctor and I knew you not?   280

GRATIANO
Were you the clerk that is to make me cuckold?

NERISSA
Ay, but the clerk that never means to do it,
Unless he live until he be a man.

BASSANIO
Sweet doctor, you shall be my bedfellow.
When I am absent, then lie with my wife.

ANTONIO
Sweet lady, you have given me life and living,
For here I read for certain that my ships
Are safely come to road.

PORTIA   How now, Lorenzo?
My clerk hath some good comforts too for you.

NERISSA
Ay, and I'll give them him without a fee.   290
There do I give to you and Jessica
From the rich Jew, a special deed of gift,
After his death, of all he dies possessed of.

LORENZO
Fair ladies, you drop manna in the way
Of starvèd people.

PORTIA   It is almost morning,
And yet I am sure you are not satisfied
Of these events at full. Let us go in,
And charge us there upon inter'gatories,

And we will answer all things faithfully.

GRATIANO

300   Let it be so. The first inter'gatory
That my Nerissa shall be sworn on is
Whether till the next night she had rather stay,
Or go to bed now, being two hours to day.
But were the day come, I should wish it dark
Till I were couching with the doctor's clerk.
Well, while I live I'll fear no other thing
So sore as keeping safe Nerissa's ring.   *Exeunt*

COMMENTARY

The Merchant of Venice contains a large number of biblical allusions. In these notes they are cited from the version that Shakespeare would hear in church, the Bishops' Bible. This was first published in 1568, and was the official translation in the English Church until its replacement by the King James version of 1611. At certain points the Geneva translation, made by English Protestant exiles during the reign of Mary and first published at Geneva in 1560, has also been quoted to illustrate an interesting verbal parallel. Shakespeare may have read this version. All biblical quotations are given in modernized spelling.

The title
The Quarto of 1600 (Q1) title-page has 'The most excellent Historie of the *Merchant of Venice*.', with running-heads 'The comicall History of | the Merchant of Venice'. The Quarto of 1619 (Q2) amends slightly to 'The Excellent History of the Merchant of Venice' on the title-page, retaining the running-heads of Q1. The Folio of 1623 has simply 'The Merchant of Venice'. George Granville (Lord Lansdowne) published his adaptation in 1701 as 'The Jew of Venice. A Comedy'.

I.1   (stage direction) *Salerio, and Solanio.* Q2 lists three characters Solanio, Salarino, and Salerio. Salarino appears to have been a mere reduplication (perhaps with additional confusion through abbreviated speech prefixes) of Salerio.

1   *I know not why I am so sad.* Antonio's unexplained melancholy has been given many explanations: that it is a relic of an earlier version adapted by Shakespeare; that it is due to the imminent parting with Bassanio;

that (a frequent explanation) it is a foreboding of the play's 'tragedy'; that melancholy is 'a malady of the rich', 'made blunt and effeminate' by luxury; that this 'want-wit' melancholy is a necessary preparation for the inexplicable levity of a 'royal merchant', normally wise and prudent, in signing such a bond as Shylock proposes.

7 *know myself* (a version of the aphorism *Nosce teipsum*, an Elizabethan commonplace and the subject of a poem by Sir John Davies in 1599)

9 *argosies* from the Italian *una nave ragusea*, a Venetian vessel, with perhaps, by false derivation, a punning allusion to the ship *Argo* (compare 'golden fleece' below). Ragusa is in fact the modern Dubrovnik on the Adriatic coast.

portly majestic

11 *pageants*. The large set-pieces in the forms of ships, castles, etc., were drawn about the streets in shows and pageants.

12 *overpeer* look down upon

13 *curtsy*. Qs give *cursie*, F *curtsie*. The bobbing motion of a small vessel in the wake of a larger.

15 *venture* (the first suggestion, to be intensified later to its climax in Shylock's caustic 'ventures . . . squandered abroad' in scene 3, of the risk or gamble involved in foreign trade)

19 *roads* anchorages

26 *flats* shoals. Compare the reference to the Goodwins in III.1.4.

27 *Andrew*. This has been explained as a reference to an Italian naval commander, Andrea Doria, and to a Spanish galleon, the *St Andrew*, captured at Cadiz in 1596.

28 *Vailing* giving sign of submission

29 *burial* burial-place

42 *bottom* ship's hold

50 *Janus* the two-countenanced deity, god of exits and

entrances, celebrated in the opening month of the calendar. There is no evidence from effigies on coins or in sculpture that the two heads differed in mood, and Shakespeare (followed by all his editors) probably conflates Janus with the double masks of comedy and tragedy.

52   *peep* laugh with half-closed eyes

56   *Nestor* (the oldest of the heroes, the type of wisdom and gravity)

    (stage direction) *Gratiano.* The name Graziano appears to have been the name for the comic *dottore* in *commedia dell'arte.* He takes it upon himself both to 'play the fool' and to make quasi-medical judgements on his friends throughout the first scene.

60   *made you merry.* Burton, in the *Anatomy of Melancholy*, declares the best cure for melancholy (like Antonio's) is 'a cup of strong drink, mirth, music, and merry company'.

61   *prevented* anticipated, gone before

67   *strange* distant

74   *respect upon* regard for

75   *They lose it that do buy it with much care.* Compare St Matthew 16.25: 'whosoever will save his life shall lose it'.

77–8   *world . . . | A stage.* Compare Jaques in *As You Like It*, 'All the world's a stage'.

79   *fool.* Gratiano may, like Launcelot later, be cast in the analogy of the buffoon; see note on line 56 above.

81–2   *liver . . . heart.* The liver was coupled with the heart and brain, as the vital organs of the body; the supposed seat of love and violent passion. Compare *Cymbeline*, V.5.14–15: 'To you, the liver, heart and brain of Britain, | By whom I grant she lives.' Sighs and groans were thought to drain blood from the heart; see *Romeo and Juliet*, III.5.59: 'Dry sorrow drinks our blood', and *A Midsummer Night's Dream*, III.2.97: 'sighs of love, that costs the fresh blood dear'.

84 *grandsire cut in alabaster*. The Q line, here repunctuated, reads

   Sit like his grandsire, cut in Alablaster?

  Memorial tablets and tombs in churches are frequently in alabaster, a sensitive stone for carving. The Q spelling 'alablaster' is common, by confusion with 'arblaster' a cross-bow man, also spelt 'alablaster'.

85 *jaundice* yellowness of the skin caused by obstruction of the bile; commonly thought to be excited by 'the more violent mental emotions'. Compare *Troilus and Cressida*, I.3.2: 'What grief hath set this jaundice o'er your cheeks?'

88 *sort* kind; band

89 *cream and mantle* cover with a pale and sour froth. Compare *King Lear*, III.4.131: 'the green mantle of the standing pool'.

92 *conceit* conception, understanding

93 *Sir Oracle*. F has 'Sir an oracle', punctuated by Granville, *Jew of Venice*, 'I am, Sir, an Oracle.' But see *The Winter's Tale*, I.2.196, 'Sir Smile, his neighbour'.

96–7 *reputed wise | For saying nothing*. See Proverbs 17.28: 'Even a fool, when he holdeth his peace, is counted wise.'

99 *call their brothers fools*. See St Matthew 5.22: 'whosoever shall say [to his brother] thou fool, shall be in danger of hell fire.'

102 *gudgeon* (a fresh-water fish – *Gobio fluviatilis* – used as bait; a gullible person)

104 *after dinner* (as the Puritan divines continued their long sermons)

110 *gear* business; or, perhaps better, nonsense-talk

112 *a neat's tongue* an ox tongue
  not vendible not marriageable

120 *pilgrimage*. The lover is exalted almost to canonization; compare II.7.40: 'To kiss this shrine, this mortal breathing saint'.

124   *something* somewhat
         port style

129   *time* young life-time

130   *gaged* pledged, as in pawn. A first anticipation of the
         Bond theme.

132   *a warranty* an authorization. A legal term (a covenant or
         undertaking in contract), extending the implication of
         'gage', as an anticipation of the Bond.

137   *the eye of honour* the scope of honour's vision

141   *of the self-same flight* of the same trajectory, size or
         weight, equally feathered

142   *advisèd* deliberate

145   *pure innocence* (the guilelessness of the 'childhood proof'
         in the previous line)

150–51   *or ... | Or* either ... or

154   *To wind about my love with circumstance* to beat about the
         bush. *Circumstance* means circumlocution.

160   *prest* ready. From Old French and the popular Latin
         praestus (modern French *prêt*); there is probably an
         overtone of 'pressed', meaning 'bound', again carrying
         a premonition of the Bond theme.

162   *fair*. This adjective begins the series continued in
         'sunny' and 'golden'. Portia is conceived as the ideal of
         the Venetian school of painting, of Titian and Giorgione,
         of a fair, red-gold hair, the colour with which Queen
         Elizabeth qualified as a fair beauty (as opposed to the
         'dark lady'). Emphasizing the contrast, Nerissa's name
         appears derived from the Italian *Nericcia* (from *nero*,
         black [-haired]). Portia is of course in the Petrarchan
         tradition; like Petrarch's Laura, she has '*biondi capelli*',
         '*cape*' *d'oro*', '*le treccie bionde Ch'oro forbito e perle Eran*
         ... a vederle' ('fair hair', 'a golden head', 'fair tresses
         which resembled rich gold and pearls').

165–6   *Portia ... Cato's daughter, Brutus' Portia*. Shakespeare
         appears to have intended her name to carry consider-
         able significance. It is possible that there is a light pun
         on 'portion', with its implication of 'inheritance' or

'dowry'. Portia, wife of Marcus Junius Brutus, conspirator with Cassius against Caesar, was the daughter of Cato Uticensis, who had gained a particular reputation for rectitude and was himself an enemy of Caesar's. Compare *Julius Caesar*, II.1.296–7: 'Think you I am no stronger than my sex, | Being so fathered, and so husbanded?'

170   *golden fleece*. Jason gathered the Argonauts who sought the Golden Fleece, finding it in Colchis and winning it with the aid of Medea, the enchantress-daughter of the King of Colchis; the latter, like Portia's father, confronted the Argonauts with a triple-test of their wit. Medea appears again in the play (V.1.13–14), when she 'did renew old Aeson', the father of Jason. Compare III.2.241: 'We are the Jasons, we have won the Fleece.'

171   *strond* strand, shore

175   *thrift*. Bassanio's quest is conceived in terms which link him with the Shylock/Laban 'way to thrive', for 'thrift is blessing if men steal it not' (I.3.87).

181   *racked* strained. With its associations with 'rack-rent' and with the instrument of torture, this passage emphasizes the darker aspect of Bassanio's squandering dependence on Antonio, which was hinted at in line 157, 'Than if you had made waste of all I have'. Both Bassanio and Antonio earn the austere Shylock's contempt as 'prodigals', with 'ventures ... squandered abroad'.

183   *presently* immediately

I.2   (stage direction) *Nerissa*. This name is probably derived from the Italian implying dark-haired (see note on I.1.162) by contrast with the golden Portia.

1   *aweary*. Portia opens the first scene in the more golden world of Belmont with an echo of Antonio's *malaise* in the first scene in Venice.

7–9   *superfluity comes sooner by white hairs, but competency lives longer*. Excess ages sooner but moderation lives longer.

10   *sentences* sententiae, aphorisms. With perhaps a light pun on the legal sense.

      pronounced delivered. This extends the legal phraseology – perhaps preparing for Portia's role in Act IV – through her next speeches, with *laws, decree, counsel, surety, sealed under*.

13   *chapels had been churches*. A chapel is frequently a portion of a large church, often separately dedicated and with its own altar; the term was also used for an outlying chapel of a principal church or monastery. Compare its use in Stratford for the Guild Chapel.

21-7   *choose ... will ... lottery*. A complex pun extends Portia's dilemma through these lines: her father's *will* (i.e. both 'choice' and 'testament') limits her personal choice; the element of chance or apparent caprice in the casket device, meriting the term 'lottery', is modified by the pun implied in that word on 'allottery'. Compare *As You Like It*, where Orlando's inheritance is described as 'the poor allottery my father left me by testament' (I.1.65).

36   *level at* aim at

37   *Neapolitan*. The Neapolitans of Shakespeare's day were especially famed for horsemanship.

38   *colt* callow, uncouth young man

43   *County Palatine*. Count occasionally (but see line 56) retains the second syllable of the French and Italian forms. The daughter of James I married a Count Palatine.

46-7   *weeping philosopher* (Heraclitus of Ephesus, about 500 B.C.) Juvenal, satirizing the 'vanity of human wishes', contrasts the laughing philosopher, Democritus, with the weeping philosopher Heraclitus (*Satire X*, 31-2, '*de sapientibus alter ridebat ... flebat contrarius alter*').

48-9   *death's-head* a *memento mori*. A 'skull and crossed bones' frequently engraved on brasses or cut on tomb-stones.

57   *throstle* thrush ('trassell' in Q and F, probably a dialect pronunciation)

69   *How oddly he is suited!* . . . Compare Greene, *Farewell to Follie* (1591): 'I have seen an English gentleman so diffused in his suits, his doublet being for the wear of Castile, his hose for Venice, his hat for France, his cloak for Germany'; and Nashe's English youth in *The Unfortunate Traveller* (1594), who 'imitated four or five sundry nations in my attire at once'.

70   *round hose* circular or puffed-out hose

72   *Scottish.* This is the Q reading; it is assumed that the F emendation to 'other lord' reflects the wish for better relations with Scotland after James's accession.

76-7   *the Frenchman became his surety.* Reference to the 'auld alliance' between Scotland and France, a constant trouble to Elizabeth. Note Portia's legal terms relating to bonds and sureties.

83-4   *best . . . beast* (punningly)

90   *Rhenish.* Compare III.1.37, where Rhenish is preferred to red wine (a judgement echoed in part in *King Lear*, I.1.258, in France's derogatory 'wat'rish Burgundy'). William Turner, describing wine drunk in England in 1568, says that 'Rhenish wine . . . is commonly a year old at the least, before it be drunken: and therefore it is older [and more potent] than the common claret wine, which dureth not commonly above one year.'

98   *imposition* command, will

100   *Sibylla* a proper name (as opposed to the 'nine sibyls' of *1 Henry VI*, I.2.56) and hence the Cumaean Sibyl of Ovid, *Metamorphoses*, XIV, who asked Apollo for the gift of long life

101   *Diana* 'Queen and huntress, chaste and fair' (Ben Jonson, 'Hymn to Diana' from *Cynthia's Revels*). Compare *1 Henry IV*, I.2.24: 'let us be Diana's foresters . . . minions of the moon'; and *A Midsummer Night's Dream*,

I.1.89: 'on Diana's altar to protest | For aye austerity and single life'.

107   *a scholar and a soldier*. Compare Ophelia's ideal 'noble mind' (*Hamlet*, III.1.151), 'The courtier's, soldier's, scholar's, eye, tongue, sword'.

108   *Marquis of Montferrat*. Nerissa could scarcely cite a more evocative family name for the scholar-soldier companion to Bassanio. The house of Monferrato was founded in 967 and for centuries struggled with Savoy for the leadership of Lombardy; it was a leading power throughout the Crusades and in 1175 inherited the kingdom of Thessalonica, a key city in the amber trade with Venice. William the Great of Monferrato in 1257 married Isabella, daughter of the Duke of Gloucester; he established an alliance with the Visconti of Milan and was the virtual creator of the *condottieri*. The family declined in the fifteenth century and by the mid six-teenth century the marquisate passed to the Dukes of Mantua.

109   *Yes, yes, it was Bassanio*. Portia answers impetuously and immediately covers up her eagerness.

124   *complexion of a devil*. Compare *Othello*, V.2.134: 'And you the blacker devil'.

125-7   *Come Nerissa ... door* (a very rough doggerel 'couplet' closing the scene)

I.3   (stage direction) *Shylock*. There are many suggestions for the derivation of the name, of which the principal are: (1) from the Hebrew 'Shallach', a cormorant, a fre-quent Elizabethan term for usurers; (2) from an obscure dialect word 'shallock', to idle or slouch. More attractive is the suggestion that it is a semi-morality term, Shy-Lock, implying secrecy and hoarding.

1   *ducats*. A ducat (literally, a piece coined by a duke or doge) is a Venetian gold piece, *Ducatus Venetorum*. Coryat estimated in 1608 that it was worth 4s. 8d. and

Cotgrave in 1632 that 'they hold a rate much about
5 or 6 shillings sterling the piece'. By any calculation of
values, therefore, three thousand ducats was a very large
(a prodigal) sum. The six to eight hundred pounds sterling to which it amounted must be multiplied by at
least twenty-five to reach a comparable sum today (i.e.
about £20,000). Some comparisons are possible in
Shakespearian terms. If Bassanio was borrowing £700
of Antonio – and hence of Shylock – Sir Hugh Evans
(*The Merry Wives of Windsor*, I.1.57) regarded such a
dowry for Anne Page as 'goot gifts'; in 1597 Shakespeare himself purchased the substantial property, New
Place, for £60; Shakespeare's annual rent for a cottage
in Rowington in 1604 was 2s. 6d.; and he bequeathed
to his daughter Judith a total of £300.

1, 6   *well*. This is assent and not a question, as some editors
have suggested.

7   *stead* 'assist' or 'supply'

12   *a good man* a dramatic ambiguity; Shylock opens up
the possibility of misunderstanding which he tactically
withdraws when Bassanio is roused. Compare *Coriolanus*, I.1.14: 'We are accounted poor citizens, the
patricians good.'

16   *sufficient* adequate surety

17   *supposition* doubt

19   *Rialto*. Both the bridge (the Ponte di Rialto) and the
Exchange or Bourse – 'an eminent place in Venice
where merchants commonly meet' (Florio, *Italian
Dictionary*, 1611).

21   *squandered*. The verb emphasizes the suggestion of
prodigality in Shylock's 'ventures' in the same line, as
it also continues his ambiguous manner, for 'squander'
may mean scatter, with no pejorative meaning.

23   *pirates*. But Q and F have 'Pyrats', sardonically extending 'land *rats* and water *rats*' in the preceding lines.

27–8   *assured* (a further sardonic emphasis, shifting the meaning from Bassanio's 'certain' to Shylock's 'guaranteed')

32   *prophet the Nazarite.* Both Jews and Mohammedans
      conceded the prophetic, though not the divine, status
      of Christ. Nazarite is a false etymology; properly it was
      a prophet under special vows (for example, Samson and
      St John Baptist); but in all the English translations of
      the Bible until 1611 it was used falsely for 'Nazarene',
      an inhabitant of Nazareth.
      conjured the devil into (the miracle of the Gadarene
      swine in St Matthew 8, St Mark 5, and St Luke 8)

34-5   *I will not eat with you, drink with you, nor pray with you.*
      Eating and drinking are for Shylock sacramental acts
      and his religious exclusiveness is equally conveyed in
      the three verbs.

38   *fawning publican* a vividly unusual term for the
      publicani, the renegade Jewish taxgatherers employed
      by ancient Rome. Two senses fit Shylock's use: his
      contempt for the penitent publican in the parable of
      St Luke 18 who desired mercy; his identification of
      Antonio with the oppressive publicans who robbed the
      Jews of 'well-won thrift'.

42-8   *usance ... thrift ... interest.* The variety of terms cor-
      responds to degrees of reprehension and excuse for a
      hated practice. Thomas, *Historye of Italye*, 1561, des-
      cribes the wealth of the Venetian Jews through usury:
      'It is almost incredible what gain the Venetians receive
      by the usury of the Jews . . . by reason whereof the
      Jews are out of measure wealthy in those parts.'
      Bacon's *Essay of Usury* (1625) declares both 'that it is
      against nature for money to beget money' and that
      'Usurers should have orange-tawny bonnets because
      they do Judaize', a pun on Judas and Judah, with a dual
      reference to the Judas-colour and the yellow cap of
      the Jewish dress in some parts of Christendom.

43   *upon the hip* (a wrestling term with a possible reference
      to the dislocation of Jacob's hip in wrestling with the
      angel in Genesis 32)

44-8   *ancient grudge ... sacred nation ... my tribe.* This is the emotional key to the relationship between Shylock and Antonio. Religious and racial pride precede commercial rivalry.

54   *Tubal*. This is clearly a biblical name, associated with Tubal-cain, a maker of instruments or weapons. The name may also have associations with alien or outcast peoples; this brings him into appropriate association with Chus (or Cush): 'his [Shylock's] countrymen' (III.2.285). Cush has certainly alien overtones, for it is the land of Ethiopia.

59   *excess*. Another pejorative word for usury, echoed by Shylock in 'advantage' at line 67 and taken up into the Belmont scenes in Portia's 'scant this excess' (III.2.112).

60   *ripe*. Furness conjectured 'rife wants', wants that come thick upon him. Johnson: 'wants that can have no longer delay'.

61   *possessed* informed. Compare *Twelfth Night*, II.3.130: 'Possess us, possess us'.

68–71 *Jacob ... wise mother ... third possessor*. This is a complex passage paraphrasing a great deal in Genesis 27 and 30. Esau should have inherited from Isaac and would therefore have been 'the third possessor' after Abraham; but Rebeccah, Jacob's 'wise mother', conspired with Jacob to cheat his blind father Isaac both of his blessing and Esau's inheritance, by putting 'the skins of kids upon his hands and upon the smooth of his neck'. Shylock's savouring of Jacob's being 'the third possessor' is both pride in his own lineage and a sardonic approval of sharp practice. Shakespeare and his contemporary readers of the Bible would be clear about the orthodox attitude to the incident, for the Geneva Bible has a marginal comment that '*this subtilty is blameworthy because [Rebeccah] should have tarried till God had performed his promise*' and the Bishops' Bible (which Shakespeare appears to have used most often) that '*Jacob was not without fault, who might have tarried until God had changed his father's mind.'* (See Introduction, pp. 12–16.)

75–85 *When Laban and himself were compromised . . . Jacob's.*
These eleven lines describe Jacob's further dubious treatment of his father-in-law Laban, and anticipate Shylock's trick with the bond. The passage echoes the language of the Bishops' Bible ('and the sheep conceived before the rods and brought forth lambs ring-straked, spotted and partie', Genesis 30.39), but the clash between Antonio and Shylock on the ambiguous morality of Jacob's action is reflected in the strained marginal glosses: the Geneva Bible has the comment, *'Jacob herein used no deceit: for it was God's commandment'* that Jacob should thrive; the Bishops' Bible is even more uneasy. *'All the increase of our labour is to be looked for at God's hand'* but *'it is not lawful by fraud to seek recompense of injury:'* (which Laban had done to Jacob) *'therefore Moses sheweth afterwards* (Genesis 31.5) *that God thus instructed Jacob.'* In the whole of this passage Shakespeare shows a striking insight into the Jewish pride in race, and a remarkable command of biblical and theological argument.

75 *compromised* in agreement
76 *eanlings* new-born lambs (from Old English *eanian,* to give birth)
82 *kind* nature
86–7 *thrive . . . thrift.* Shylock describes Jacob's sharp practice in the language of thrift which was used by the Puritans to account for their worldly success through moral uprightness.
88 *venture.* Antonio's riposte to Shylock's 'ventures . . . squandered'.
93 *breed.* See Introduction, pp. 12–13.
99 *goodly outside.* The contrast between appearance and reality is a Shakespearian commonplace; it is central to the casket scenes later.
106 *patient shrug* (a semitic gesture; compare *The Jew of*

Malta, II.3.24: 'Heave up my shoulder when they call
me dog'.)

107   *badge*. The literal significance is much debated; Booth
wrote in his published acting-version: 'I prefer the
yellow cap [Bacon's 'orange-tawny bonnet'] to the
cross upon the shoulder which other actors have worn,
my Father among them. Cooke used the cap, and said
that Macklin also used it.' (See Introduction, p. 46,
and note on line 109.)

108   *misbeliever* a very precise term. A Jew was not an
*un*believer, an atheist or an infidel, but a *mis*believer,
one who believes wrongly or heretically. See the collect
for Good Friday, recited until recently in varying
forms in both the Anglican and the Roman use: 'Have
mercy upon all Jews, Turks, Infidels, and Heretics.'

109   *Jewish gaberdine*. Vecellio's treatise on costume (1590)
makes no distinction in the dress of Jew and Christian
except the yellow cap; the *gavardina* was simply a
peasant's cloak. Stage tradition may be echoed in
Jordan's ballad *The Forfeiture* (1664):

> *His habit was a Jewish gown,*
> *That would defend all weather;*

for after 1412 all Moors and Jews in Spain had to wear
such a long cloak, which came to their feet.

120   *bondman*. Compare 'purchased slave' in the Trial
scene, IV.1.90.

131   *breed of barren metal*. Q has 'breed for'. Commentators
have boggled at the antithesis 'breed – barren', Theobald
suggesting 'bearing metal' and Pope 'bribe of . . .' Lord
Lansdowne's *The Jew of Venice*, 1701, has 'A Breed of
sordid Mettal'. The passage in fact reflected the normal
attitude of the playwrights to usury, that it was 'against
nature'.

137   *doit* a trifle; a Dutch coin (*duit*) 'whereof eight go to
a stiver, and ten stivers do make our English shilling'
(Coryat, 1611)

139   *This is kind I offer.* 'Kind' is a pun on its two possible meanings, the noun 'nature' and the adjective 'generous'.

141   *notary* (a clerk specifically authorized to draw up contracts)

142   *single bond.* This seems to imply a *simplex obligatio*, a promise to pay without conditions attached. But this bond is precisely different, has conditions annexed and Shylock would appear to be deceitfully playing down its graver implications to the level of his 'merry sport'.

146   *nominated for* named as

    equal pound precise or just weight. This ironically prepares for Portia's quibble, 'nor cut thou less nor more | But just a pound of flesh' (IV.1.322–3).

147   *fair flesh* (possibly an ironic contrast between the fair Venetian and the darker, oriental Shylock)

171   *purse the ducats straight.* At the beginning of the scene Shylock purported to depend on Tubal for part of the sum.

175   *The Hebrew will turn Christian* (a climax of irony in an ironic scene, anticipating the judgement on Shylock)

    kind (a final use of the pun, several times repeated in this scene, playing on 'kindness' and 'nature')

178   *My ships come home* (a hubristic tempting of chance and fate, the venture which Shylock despised)

II.1   (stage direction) *the Prince of Morocco, a tawny Moor.* Shakespeare portrays two other Moors, Aaron in *Titus Andronicus* and Othello. In all three characters there is a concern with the dark skin, but in *The Merchant of Venice* and *Othello* the Moor is a figure of conscious dignity and nobility. Morocco was a tawny-Moor as opposed to a 'Blackamoor'. Compare Aaron (*Titus Andronicus*, V.1.27), who is a 'tawny slave', and Raleigh's phrase 'The Negro's which we call the Blacke-Mores'.

    accordingly matching, in accord

2   *shadowed livery* a heraldic term for a shaded or umbrated device or cognizance. Since 'umbrated' means
'drawn in outline', allowing the true colour of the 'field'
to show through, Morocco implies that his dark skin is
mere outline or superficial appearance, allowing the
true colour of his blood to show through.

7   *reddest* a sign of martial valour and dignity. Furness
cites the Old English custom of colours for palls or
hearse-cloths: 'The red of valiancy ... kings, lords,
knights and valiant soldiers: white over clergymen, in
token of their profession and honest life, and over
virgins and matrons.'

8   *aspect* look, visage (accented on the second syllable)

9   *feared* frightened

13   *In terms of* in way of

14   *nice direction* scrupulous guidance

17   *scanted* limited

18   *wit* wisdom

20   *fair* (an allusion to the early play on the colours, tawny,
white and red)

25   *Sophy* Emperor of Persia

26   *Sultan Solyman.* In 1535 the Sultan Suleiman conducted an unsuccessful campaign against Persia. The
two lines would seem to indicate that Morocco was one
of Suleiman's commanders.

27   *o'erstare* outstare (the reading of Q2). Compare 'overpeer' in I.1.12.

29   *she-bear.* The bear in Shakespeare is among the most
cruel aspects of nature. See *King Lear*, III.4.10: 'if thy
flight lay toward the roaring sea | Thou'dst meet the
bear i'th'mouth', and *The Winter's Tale*, III.3, where
sea and bear vie in cruelty.

32   *Lichas* an attendant on Hercules (Alcides); hence the
emendation of Q and F 'rage' in line 35 to 'page'.
Lansdowne alters the passage, assigning it to Bassanio:
'So were a Gyant worsted by a Dwarf.'

       dice. This game of chance focuses the word-play

throughout this scene on the hazard of the casket choice: *lott'ry, destiny, blind Fortune, chance, hazard, Good fortune.*

II.2 (stage direction) *Launcelot Gobbo*. Shakespeare seems to have intended a family of comic hump-backs, from the Italian '*gobba*', a hump, and '*gobbo*', hunchbacked. Jacques Callot (1592–1635) engraved two series of *commedia dell'arte* types, the *Balli di Sfessania* and the *Gobbi* or hunchbacks.

1–2 *conscience . . . fiend*. Launcelot participates in a dramatic morality, the medieval tradition of quasi-dramatic dialogue on a moral theme.

9 *Fia* (a form of 'via' – away!)

15–16 *smack . . . grow to . . . taste* a flavour (of lechery). To 'grow to' was applied to burnt milk sticking to a pan.

24 *incarnation*. Q2 reads 'incarnall'. Compare Mistress Quickly's malapropism in *Henry V*, II.3.34: 'carnation . . . a colour he never liked'. 'Carnation colours' in miniature paintings were the flesh tones.

28 (stage direction) *Old Gobbo*. See first note to this scene.

32–3 *sand-blind, high-gravel-blind* (as opposed to stone-blind or totally blind)

33 *try confusions*. A malapropism for 'try conclusions' (which is the reading of Q2).

40 *sonties* saints (from Old French or the Scottish 'zauntie')

43 *Master* (a term of some dignity applied to the rank of esquire, or to an employer as opposed to a servant)

48 *well to live* comfortable, well to do. This expands in a punning form, a comment on 'poor' in the previous line.

52 *ergo* therefore

57–8 *Sisters Three* (the Fates)

86 *what a beard*. This depends on the traditional stage business of Launcelot's kneeling for blessing with his back to Old Gobbo. It is possible that this 'recognition' by his hairiness at the point of receiving a blessing picks

up ironically Shylock's reference to Jacob's trick in
I.3.70, where Jacob, the 'smooth man', is mistaken for
Esau by assuming the hairy skin of kids. (See note to
I.3.68–71.)

88   *fill-horse* (a draught-horse in the 'fills' or shafts)

96   *set up my rest* made up my mind

111   *Gramercy* God reward you greatly (Old French, *grant
merci*)

115   *infection* (malapropism for 'affection', i.e. inclination)

120   *cater-cousins* (perhaps from 'cater', to provide for; that
is, a dependant but no blood-relation)

123   *frutify* (for 'certify')

126   *impertinent* (for 'pertinent')

132   *defect* (for 'effect', import)

134   *Shylock thy master spoke with me.* This is a strange incident in the relationship between Bassanio and Shylock.

135   *preferred.* Preferment, in the sense of advancement, is
now most frequently used of clerical advancement.

138–40 *The old proverb is very well parted* ... Launcelot parts
or divides the proverb between his old and new master:
'The grace of God is gear enough', that is, Bassanio has
the 'grace of God' and Shylock has 'enough' – a competency in wealth.

144   *guarded.* Guards are the frogs or braids on a uniform or
livery. Bassanio on his borrowings is fitting out a rich
retinue ('rare new liveries', line 101 above), but Launcelot's coat is to be more heavily braided than the
others. There is perhaps a suggestion of a fool's 'motley
coat guarded with yellow' (*Henry VIII*, Prologue,
line 16).

147   *table* (the palm of the hand between the 'line of fortune'
and the 'natural line')

149   *line of life* (the circular line at the base of the thumb)

154   *gear* business

155–6 *twinkling.* Q2 extends to 'twinkling of an eye'.

158   *bestowed* stowed in the hold (of the ship bound for
Belmont)

165   *suit to* a boon to beg of (but see note to line 177)

172   *liberal.* Gratiano's qualities ('Parts') are too licentious for the delicate embassy of Bassanio.

175   *misconstered* misconstrued

177   *sober habit.* The theme of outward appearance is advanced in this scene by the play on garments and liveries. Gratiano's 'suit' (wish) is punningly extended on an ironic parallel to Launcelot. Later in the speech he will '*look* demurely', use '*observance* of civility' and study a 'sad ostent' (an outward show of gravity). To all this Bassanio responds at line 188 that he should rather, for the moment, 'put on | Your boldest suit of mirth', completing the play on *suit.*

II.3   (stage direction) *Jessica.* It seems difficult to associate Jessica with the Iscah or Iesca of Genesis 11.29. If her name is so derived, it may also, from a Hebrew root, carry implications of treachery or spying.

10   *exhibit* (perhaps another malapropism for 'inhibit', or, with unwonted literacy, 'my tears demonstrate what my tongue would say')

II.4.1   *supper-time.* There is to be a masque at the meal, like the Masque of the Senses at Timon's supper (*Timon of Athens*, Act I).

2   *Disguise.* They will be either 'visored' with small masks, or dressed in character.

5   *spoke us yet* bespoken or given orders for. F4 amends to 'spoke as yet'.

      torchbearers (a regular feature of masques)

6   *quaintly* curiously or elegantly

10   *An* if

      break up open (the seal)

34   *gentle.* A pun on 'Gentile' as contrast to the 'faithless Jew', her father (line 37).

II.5   (stage direction) *Launcelot, his man that was, the Clown.*
There is possibly a suggestion here that Launcelot has
ceased to be a 'natural' and become a professional
clown, donning the motley.

17–18 *There is some ill a-brewing towards my rest* ... Dreams
were ambiguous, sometimes revealing direct truth,
sometimes by contraries.

20   *reproach* (for 'approach', a 'feed' line for Shylock's
sardonic reply)

24   *a-bleeding* (perhaps ominous)
Black Monday (the day after Easter, equated in Laun-
celot's deliberate nonsense with the penitential Ash
Wednesday)

29   *wry-necked fife.* The fife has no curved mouth-piece but
the player is described in Barnaby Rich's *Irish Hubbub*
(1616): 'a fife is a wry-necked musician, for he always
looks away from his instrument'.

32   *varnished faces.* The masquers were made up with the
thoroughness of Elizabethan cosmetic art described in
the ironic by-play between Viola and Olivia in *Twelfth
Night*, I.5.220–27. Faces were painted with 'pencils'
(fine brushes) with the 'carnation' tones of red and
white 'truly blent'. This staining of the skin ('in grain')
merited the term 'varnish'; *Timon of Athens*, a play
much concerned with 'deceitful appearance', has
the term 'painted, like his varnished friends' (IV.2.36).

34–5   *foppery* ... *sober house.* Shylock has a constant ten-
dency to a grave puritanism which may seem 'hell' to
Jessica or the 'merry devil', Launcelot.

35   *Jacob's staff.* From Genesis 32.10: 'With my staff
came I over this Jordan, and now have I gotten two
companies.' The gravity of Shylock's 'sober house' is
carried on in his reference to Jacob's staff, which was
the measure of his power when he crossed Jordan with
his little band ('*that is, poor and without all provision*'
in the Geneva Bible margin). To Elizabethan ears there
would be a further religious ambiguity in Shylock's

possible reference to the staff of those who went on
pilgrimage to the shrine of St James (Jacobus) of
Compostella.

41   *Jewess' eye.* Q and F have 'Jewes', F3 'Jew's' and Pope
first conjectures 'Jewess' '. 'A Jew's eye' was proverbial
for excessive value.

42   *Hagar's offspring.* Ishmael, the son of Hagar 'the bond-
woman' to Sarah, wife of Abraham, is described
(Genesis 16.12) as 'a wild man' (in the Geneva Bible
margin: '*Or, fierce and cruel, or, as a wild ass*');
Shylock wryly identifies Launcelot both with the rebel-
lious Ishmael and with servile descent from Abraham,
as opposed to Isaac the free born.

44   *patch* fool. Sir Thomas Wilson, *Art of Rhetoric* (1585):
'Patch or Coulson ... these two in their time were
notable fools.' But perhaps from Italian *pazzo*, a fool
(Latin *fatuus*).

45   *profit* improvement (in learning rather than in wealth)

II.6.2   *hour* appointed time

5–7   *O ten times faster Venus' pigeons fly | To seal love's bonds
new-made than they are wont | To keep obligèd faith un-
forfeited.* The doves of Venus attend a betrothal more
readily than they assist a lasting marriage.

5   *Venus' pigeons* the doves which drew Venus's chariot

10   *untread* retrace

14   *younger* a younger son, precisely equivalent to the
prodigal in the same line. Rowe unnecessarily emended
to *younker*, a young nobleman.

15   *scarfèd* under full sail or possibly 'dressed overall' (but
see note to line 18)

16   *strumpet wind* (like the harlots of the Prodigal parable,
St Luke 15)

18   *With overweathered ribs* with starting timbers, springing
apart at the joints (unlike the sound, well-jointed hull,
which may be the meaning of 'scarfèd' in line 15)

21   *abode* delay

23   *thieves* (the first dark suggestion of stealth in the elopement)

35   *exchange* (an ironic term which refers to her disguise as a boy, her abandonment of Shylock and her theft of jewels and money, with the play's prevailing overtones of commerce)

37   *pretty* artful (in a pejorative sense)

41–2   *candle . . . light.* Light had frequently the sense 'flippant' or 'wanton'; see V.1.130: 'a light wife doth make a heavy husband'.

43   *discovery* (a military term)

45   *garnish* decoration (yet again with overtones of deceitful appearance)

49   *gild* carry more gold. This extends the sense of 'varnish' in relation to the masquers; compare Lady Macbeth: 'I'll gild the faces of the grooms withal, | For it must seem their guilt' (II.2.56–7).

51   *by my hood* (an oath by his masque habit, or, ironically, by a monk's hood)
       a gentle and no Jew (a repetition of the pun on 'Gentile')

II.7.1 *discover* reveal

11   *contains my picture.* Compare this with the statement to Bassanio (III.2.40): 'I am locked in one of them', and to Arragon (II.9.5): 'I am contained'.

19   *advantages* increase or interest. In his rejection of 'shows of dross' the noble Morocco may seem to be rejecting mercenary Venice.

30   *disabling* disparagement

40   *kiss this shrine, this mortal breathing saint.* By the conventions of courtly love, the lady is an object of veneration, like a saint or holy object within a reliquary.

41   *Hyrcanian.* Hyrcania was south of the Caspian and as the breeding-ground of tigers was scarcely a 'through-

fare'. Compare the Hyrcan(ian) tigers of *Macbeth*, III.4.100, and *Hamlet*, II.2.444.

50   *base . . . gross*. Lead is both a base metal and crude.

51–2   *rib . . . immured*. These funereal terms anticipate the 'carrion Death' which is Morocco's reward.

51   *cerecloth* (the waxed sheet in which the body was embalmed before being enclosed in lead for burial)

53   *ten times undervalued* (the precise comparative valuation of silver to gold)

56   *angel* a gold coin, with the device of the archangel Michael treading down the dragon. The association of England with 'angels' was a regular pun from St Augustine of Canterbury to Shakespeare.

57   *insculped* engraved. In Richard Robinson's version of the *Gesta Romanorum* (1577), a possible source for this play (see Introduction, p. 18), a lead vessel is 'insculpt' with a posy. Shakespeare uses the word nowhere else. It should perhaps be pointed out that he does, however, use 'insculpture', in *Timon of Athens*, V.4.67.

61   *form* image. A neo-platonic term and involved with the suggestion of substance, reality and appearance (see note on line 11 above).

63   *carrion Death* (a skull or *memento mori*)

69   *Gilded tombs*. Q and F have 'gilded timber', Sonnet 101 'gilded tomb'; compare the Geneva Bible version of St Matthew 23.27, 'For ye are like unto whited tombs, which appear beautiful outward, but are within full of dead men's bones,' and the Bishops' Bible, 'like unto painted sepulchres'.

75   *farewell heat* (an inversion of the 'farewell frost' found for example in Wapull's *Tyde Taryeth No Man*, 1576, and Lyly's *Mother Bombie*)

79   *complexion* both 'appearance' and 'temperament'

II.8.4   *The Duke* [of Venice]. The title *Doge* has become customary in English usage and this figure is familiar to us from the many admirable portraits of Dukes of Venice.

15 *ducats . . . daughter*. Compare *The Jew of Malta*, II.1.54: 'O girl! O gold! O beauty! O my bliss!' Note that we have only Solanio's report for this ridiculous outburst by Shylock; his grief on stage is never visible.

25 *keep his day* fulfil his bond. Compare 'break his day' above (I.3.160).

27 *reasoned* talked

28 *the narrow seas* (the English Channel)

39 *Slubber* carry out carelessly, scamp. Compare its sense of 'smear' in *Othello*, I.3.227: 'slubber the gloss of your new fortunes'.

44 *ostents* appearances

II.9.1–3 *Quick . . . straight . . . presently* (a hurried immediacy to rid Belmont of Arragon)

5 *I am contained*. Compare II.7.11 and III.2.40.

13 *marriage* (pronounced with three syllables)

14 *Lastly* (a two-syllable line)

26 *fool* (adjectival here)

27 *fond* foolish

28 *the martlet* a swift (which builds in insecure places)

30 *force and road* (conjectured to translate *in vi et via*, exposed to the attack of)

32 *jump* agree

38 *cozen* deceive

39 *stamp* seal, mark

41 *estates, degrees, and offices* positions, ranks, and functions

44 *cover* wear their hats

49 *new varnished* outward adornment (as elsewhere in this play)

51 *assume* claim

61 *To offend and judge are distinct offices*. Arragon cannot be tried and be a judge in his own cause.

63   *Seven times trièd* purified seven times by heat. Compare the significance of quintessence, distilled five times.

66   *shadows kiss* kiss a portrait (the shadow or counterfeit of the original sitter)

68   *iwis* truly (a word to fill the line)

71   *your head* a fool's head (where he should be the head of the household). Compare Ephesians 5.23, 'The husband is the head of the wife.'

78   *wroth* ruth (misfortune) rather than wrath (Q and F wroath)

89   *sensible regreets* substantial greetings, i.e. gifts

90   *commends* commendations
         breath speech

98   *high-day* holiday. Compare St John 19.31, 'for that Sabbath day was an high day', and *The Merry Wives of Windsor*, III.2.59, 'he speaks holiday'.

100   *post* messenger

101   *Bassanio Lord, love if thy will it be!* The reading of Q and F, to be paraphrased 'Lord Bassanio, love if you will (for Portia will respond)'. Rowe's conjectural punctuation 'Bassanio, Lord Love', addresses the Cupid of the previous line, that is, 'Cupid, may this newcomer be Bassanio.'

III.1.2   *unchecked* unconfirmed or uncontradicted (probably the latter)

5   *flat* shallows

6   *gossip* godmother (but here 'Dame' as a title)

9   *knapped* nibbled. The verb means to cut short or break, from the Dutch, *knappen*. Compare Psalms 46.9: 'he... knappeth the spear in sunder.'
         ginger (probably 'ginger-snaps' rather than the tough root-ginger)

11   *slips* cuttings or scions. Compare *The Winter's Tale*, IV.4.99: 'I'll not put | The dibble in earth to set one slip of them'.

15   *the full stop* the 'stop' or halt in the manage of a trained horse. (Solanio's tongue is running away.)

19–20   *cross my prayer* make the sign of the cross at the end of a prayer (with a play on 'crossing a path'). Compare *Hamlet*, I.1.127: 'I'll cross it, though it blast me.'

27   *fledged* fit to fly (Q has 'flidge')
    complexion quality or nature

31–2   *flesh and blood ... carrion*. Solanio purports to mis-understand Shylock's reference to Jessica as a reference to his own fleshly nature (carrion).

37   *red wine and Rhenish*. See note to I.2.90.

40   *match* bargain

42   *smug* 'trim' or 'complacent'
    mart market (the Rialto)

49   *disgraced me* done me disfavour

53   *I am a Jew*. Once again Shakespeare restores the balance in Shylock's character, making racial dignity a greater motive-force than commercial greed. This has been a high point in most performances. Of Edmund Kean's speaking these words Hazlitt says that he was 'worth a wilderness of monkeys that have aped humanity'.

64   *sufferance* patience. See the note at IV.1.198 for the contrasts between patience and revenge.

72   *Tubal*. The scene following is destroyed if Tubal's role is the grotesque baiting of Shylock. There is the utmost flexibility in Shylock's tone, from the resignation of 'Why there, there, there, there!' to the near-tragic deprivation of 'I had it of Leah when I was a bachelor.' Taken with this seriousness, despite its grotesque moments, this scene provides the proper context for the insight that commercial loss was a part of the nation's curse, for '*I* never felt it till now.'

81   *hearsed* coffined. Jessica, by her marriage to a Gentile, would be dead to her race and family, to say nothing of her treachery and theft.

86–8   *Nor no ill luck stirring but what lights o'my shoulders, no sighs but o'my breathing, no tears but o'my shedding*. In these three lines the rhythms of the prose intensify. At the Stratford-upon-Avon production in 1962 Peter O'Toole emphasized these rhythms by beating his breast at every repetition of 'my'. At their formal mourning, Jews accompany the ritualized wailing by beating the breast until tears are shed.

111   *turquoise*. The F and Q 'Turkies' reflects Elizabethan (and later) pronunciation. The turquoise was a natural stone for a betrothal ring (though it was semi-precious, unlike the 'seld-seen' jewels of Barabas, the Jew of Malta), for it was said 'to reconcile man and wife' and faded or brightened with the wearer's health.

116   *fee me an officer* engage a Sheriff's officer – a catchpole (to make the arrest of Antonio)

119   *synagogue*. This is to prepare 'the oath in heaven' which Shylock cannot break at the trial. Again the profoundest springs in Shylock's motivation are touched: Victor Hugo makes the appropriate comment: 'In entering his synagogue Shylock entrusts his hatred to the safeguard of his Faith. Henceforward his vengeance assumes a consecrated character. His bloodthirstiness against the Christian becomes sacerdotal.'

III.2.4   *but it is not love*. A half-prevarication, like her 'Bassanio, as I think, so was he called' (I.2.109–10).

8   *a maiden hath no tongue but thought*. Either a reference to the proverb 'Maidens should be seen and not heard' or a parallel to Rosalind's 'Do you not know I am a woman ? When I think, I must speak' (*As You Like It*, III.2.234). The ambiguities and hesitancies throughout her speech dramatically show her dilemma between her father's will and her love.

10   *I could teach you* (a possible preparation for the song. See note to line 62 below)

15   *o'erlooked me* looked at me with the evil eye (a term from witchcraft, but here used playfully)

18-19   *these naughty times | Puts bars between the owners and
        their rights* these wicked times cheat owners of their
        proper possessions

22   *piece*. Q and F 'peize', usually explained as derived
        from Old French *peser*, to retard by hanging weights;
        compare *Richard III*, V.3.105: 'Lest leaden slumber
        peise me down tomorrow'. But Rowe suggested the
        verb 'to piece', which better answers to 'eke', 'draw
        out', and 'stay' in the next two lines.

23   *eke*. The two words 'piece' and 'eke' occur in the
        Prologues to *Henry V*. In the Prologue to Act I: 'Piece
        out our imperfections', and to Act III: 'eke out our
        performance'.

29   *fear* to be apprehensive of (lest his love should not
        succeed)

32   *rack*. Silvayn's *Orator* (1596), from which Shakespeare
        may have taken hints for the Bond plot, has several
        instances of torture on the rack which produced false
        confessions of guilt. Dr Lopez (see Introduction,
        p. 8) 'pleaded . . . he had much belied himself in his
        confession to save himself from racking'.

40   *I am locked in one of them* (referring to Portia's portrait)

43-53   *Let music sound while he doth make his choice* . . . This
        speech is one of the most elaborate analyses of stage
        music in Shakespeare, drawing attention to the drama-
        tic and emotional significance of the song while Bas-
        sanio chooses. It proceeds to a formal division of the
        music's significance: if Bassanio fails he will have his
        swan-song (compare *King John*, V.7.21-2: 'faint swan |
        Who chants a doleful hymn to his own death'); if suc-
        cessful it will be a 'flourish' or fanfare at the moment
        of a royal crowning; throughout it will be both a lover's
        aubade or dawn-song ('in break of day') and an *epi-
        thalamium* or marriage-song (for the 'bridegroom's ear').

55   *Alcides* Hercules. A further reference to the choice as
        Herculean (compare Morocco's choice, II.1.35). Portia
        speaks of Bassanio's 'more love', since Hercules rescued

Hesione for a material reward, the horses which King
Laomedon of Troy, her father, had promised (Ovid,
Metamorphoses, VII, lines 237–9: 'His daughter . . . stout
Hercules delivering safe and sound, | Required his
steeds which were the hire for which he did compound').
The contrast of love and palpable reward is an ironic
comment on Bassanio's initial motive, the 'golden fleece'.

58   *Dardanian* Trojan

59   *blearèd* tear-blotched

62   (stage direction) *A song the whilst Bassanio comments.*
A much-discussed stage direction. Portia has declared
(lines 10–11) that she 'could teach you | How to choose
right'. Ingenious suggestions concerning the rhymes
'bred', 'head' etc. with 'lead' argue that the song is a
'broad hint'. The argument is in fact more delicate. It is
given an elaborate context (see lines 43–53); the song
itself is a precise account of the death of 'fancy' which is
a superficial concern with outward appearance, and dies
in the cradle, the eyes; finally, at line 73, Bassanio in
the single word 'So' links his meditations on the three
caskets with the argument of the song. This is an alto-
gether subtler texture of meaning than a mere hint from
Portia to Bassanio, which would belittle both their
relationship and her good faith. (See Introduction,
pp. 50–54.)

75   *In law.* It is characteristic of the tenor of the play that
Bassanio's first example should be legal.
    tainted evil-tasting, like stale meat, which must be
'seasoned' (line 76) by spices to make it palatable.
Compare *Much Ado about Nothing*, IV.1.142–3: 'salt
too little which may season give | To her foul tainted
flesh'.

81   *simple* palpable, uncomplicated

83–4   *false* | *As stairs of sand.* Probably 'as treacherous as steps
cut in a sand-hill'; 'bulwarks of sand', echoing the
Q and F spelling 'stayers', in the sense of 'prop, support
or stay' is also suggested.

86   *livers white as milk.* Compare *2 Henry IV*, IV.3.107–9:
        'blood ... cold and settled, left the liver white and
        pale, which is the badge of pusillanimity and coward-
        ice'.

87   *excrement* outward growth, excrescence

89   *purchased by the weight* (in the form of cosmetics)

92   *crispèd snaky golden locks.* Courtesans were regularly
        painted by the Venetian painters of the Renaissance
        with crimped gold hair; see Carpaccio's *The Courtesans*
        in the Museo Correr, Venice.

96   *sepulchre.* Compare Sonnet 68, a description of 'beauty's
        dead fleece':

> *Before the golden tresses of the dead,*
> *The right of sepulchres, were shorn away*
> *To live a second life on second head ...*

97   *guilèd* treacherous. F2 reads 'guilded'.

99   *Indian beauty* dark beauty (as opposed to the Eliza-
        bethan ideal)

103   *drudge* mere servant of exchange and commerce

108–13 Portia's response is given both intensity and aesthetic
        control by being bounded within three rhymed couplets.

112   *rain.* Either 'weep tears of joy in moderation' or, if the
        'raine' of Q and F and the 'reine' of Q 3 indicate the
        modern English 'rein', as Dr Johnson conjectured, then
        it is a term from the manage of horses and implies 'Do
        not allow your joy to run away with you.'
        excess. A term of usury which punningly extends the
        mercantile theme into that of personal relations; 'the
        rent that's due to love'. (See Introduction, p. 58.)

115   *counterfeit* portrait. There was a constant ambiguity in
        the Elizabethan aesthetic of portraiture. Likeness was
        prized but it was also (as *Timon of Athens* demonstrates
        in the conflict between the Poet and the Painter) regarded
        as a 'conceit deceitful'. The ambiguous undertone in
        'counterfeit' hints at the prevailing concern that appear-
        ance shall match reality; compare these phrases in

Timon of Athens: 'a pretty mocking of the life', 'It tutors Nature ... livelier than life', 'The painting is almost the natural man', 'Thou draw'st a counterfeit | Best in all Athens'. (See Introduction, pp. 36-8.)

127-8 *substance ... shadow*. The concern for reality behind the superficial is in these words given a neo-platonic expression.

131 *choose not by the view*. The argument is here locked up. Unlike those who have chosen by external appearance, Bassanio chooses by quality and not by mere sight.

140 *by note* by a bill of dues (a commercial term). With affectionate irony Bassanio, like Portia in line 112, transports terms of commerce into love.

148 *confirmed, signed, ratified* further legal-commercial terms. This by-play, half jest, half earnest, uniting the two main aspects of the play, is extended in the mathematical terms of Portia's next speech, lines 153-8: 'trebled twenty times', 'your account', 'sum', 'in gross', with the significant interpolation: 'virtues, beauties, *livings*, friends', where 'livings' implies possessions, tenures (as in the ecclesiastical sense).

153-5 *I would be trebled twenty times myself* ... The reading here follows the lineation in the first Quarto, the third line being an alexandrine. Some editors re-align to place the alexandrine one line earlier:

I would be trebled twenty times myself,
A thousand times more fair, ten thousand times more rich,
That only to stand high in your account ...

The extra syllables weaken the powerful duplication of number in line 154, 'A thousand times ... ten thousand times'. The Q reading gives the actor a characteristic run-on between lines 154 and 155, and the pause after 'more rich' retains the feeling of a blank-verse line in the words that follow.

158 *sum of something*. The Q reading; F has 'sum of nothing'. In either reading it is a diffident setting aside of her

wealth and a concentration on her youth, with the determination (like Katherine the Shrew) to take her husband as her lord.

167 *converted* (a final momentary return to the commercial; the converting of funds from one owner to another)

171–3 *ring . . . ruin of your love*. In the serio-comic tone of the scene, the ring could have a significance similar to that of Othello's handkerchief. It is delicately related to the potential tragedy of Antonio's trial and finally turned aside in the closing speech of the play in an inoffensive indecency.

181–2 *something . . . nothing* (a playful echo of Portia's 'sum of something')

198 *mistress . . . maid*. It is important to estimate the social distinction with nicety: Nerissa, like Maria in *Twelfth Night*, is a 'waiting-gentlewoman', no common servant, and therefore wholly worthy to marry a gentleman.

199– *intermission | No more pertains to me, my lord, than you.*
200 I, my lord, have no more escaped than you (a mock-rueful jest).

215 *stake down*. A wager (with a lewd pun implied).

218 *infidel*. This return to Jessica is a reminder of the religious undertone conveyed in 'misbeliever . . . infidel . . . Jew . . . become a Christian'.

221 *my new interest here*. Bassanio's language cannot remain long divorced from the commercial.

223 *very* veritable, true

236 *estate* (both 'condition' and 'fortune')

237 *stranger* alien (a further emphasis on Jessica's status)

239 *royal merchant* a merchant prince. In Elizabeth's day Gresham, the most notable merchant-banker of the age, was given this title.

241 *We are the Jasons, we have won the Fleece*. With a punning return to the unabashed self-aggrandizement with which Bassanio first set out on his Belmont venture, he prepares the irony of the pun 'fleece – fleets' between this line and the next.

243   *shrewd* evil, misfortunate. Compare beshrew, beshrow, used playfully throughout.

246–7   *the constitution | Of any constant man* the temper of a man whose blood and judgement were well mingled

262   *mere* sheer, absolute. Compare Queen Elizabeth's boast to her people that she was 'mere English'.

267   *hit* (the mark, an echo of Bassanio's archery analogy in the first scene)

278   *impeach the freedom of the state* imperil the freedom and equity of Venetian law

280   *magnificoes* (the Venetian rulers under the Doge)

282   *envious* malicious

285   *countrymen.* Jessica's reference to two members of her father's race and her own as his 'countrymen' has an alien sound. Shylock's term is 'tribe'.

295   *ancient Roman honour* 'antique Roman', 'high Roman fashion' – the type of stoical dignity and honour, and a term of commendation for Dane, Egyptian, or Venetian

303   *church.* The vow in II.1.44 is taken in 'the temple'; the sacrament of marriage here in 'church'.

312   *cheer* appearance, countenance

III.3   This short scene has a passionate intensity. The character of Shylock, implacable now, with religious sanctions ('I have sworn an oath', line 5) matures towards its greatest complexity.

9   *naughty* wicked
        fond foolish

20   *bootless* hopeless, unavailing

22   *forfeiture* (process of debt when a bond became forfeit)

26   *deny* prevent

27   *commodity* traffic, commercial relations (on the ease and propriety of which the wealth of Venice depended)

32   *bated* reduced. Compare its use in 'bated breath'.

III.4 (stage direction) *Balthasar*. The verse appears to demand the pronunciation Balthasár (or Bálthasar).

2 *conceit* conception

3 *godlike amity*. Lorenzo refers to a discussion in full flight between himself and Portia. She has admitted, despite the depth of her love for Bassanio, the profound claim of platonic love or friendship between Bassanio and Antonio.

9 *customary bounty* 'your accustomed goodness' (*bonté*) or 'the acts of kindness demanded by the custom or manners of gentility'

12 *waste* spend

13 *equal* (Q and F 'egall', from French '*égal*', i.e. matched, equivalent)

15 *lineaments* 'features' or, more probably, 'temperamental qualities'

20 *semblance* image, exact correspondence of. Compare 'semblable' in *Timon of Athens*, IV.3.22: 'His semblable, yea, himself, Timon disdains.'

25 *husbandry and manage* stewardship and management. 'To husband' is still used in a frugal sense; see *Macbeth*, II.1.4–5: 'There's husbandry in heaven: | Their candles are all out.'

31 *monastery*. There was in fact a Benedictine Convent near the river Brenta on the road between Padua and Venice; in this area the magnificoes of Venice had many country residences.

49 *Padua*. Q and F read 'Mantua', an error, since it disagrees with IV.1.109 and V.1.268, and Padua was the centre of Civil Law studies in Italy.

52 *imagined* all imaginable

53 *traject*. Q and F read 'tranect', probably a compositor's misreading of a manuscript 'traiect', probably from Italian *traghetto*, a ferry, found in Florio's *World of Words* (1598); and Coryat notes the 'thirteen ferries or passages [in Venice] which they commonly call Traghetti'. Twenty miles from Padua, on the Brenta, there

is a dam to control the waters short of the Venetian marshes; this may have constituted a ferry, or bridge, known to Shakespeare by travellers' hearsay.

61   *accomplishèd* equipped
69   *quaint* ingenious
72   *I could not do withal* I could not help it
77   *Jacks* contemptible fellows

III.5.1   *sins of the father.* A constant theme of Jewish theological history: 'The fathers have eaten a sour grape and the children's teeth are set on edge'; see the note below at IV.1.203.

3   *fear you* fear for you
4   *agitation* (for cogitation?)
4–5   *be o'good cheer.* Very near blasphemy, in quoting the claim of salvation in a sentence of damnation: 'Be of good cheer, I have overcome the world' (St John 16.33).
14–15   *Scylla ... Charybdis* (the cave of Scylla and the whirlpool of Charybdis, the Straits of Messina)
17   *saved by my husband.* Compare St Paul, 1 Corinthians 7.14: 'the unbelieving wife is sanctified by the husband'.
20   *enow* enough
29   *are out* have quarrelled
49–50   *cover ... duty* (a play on covered dishes in preparation for dinner and the head covered as a sign of rank)
58   *humours and conceits* literally 'inclinations and thoughts', but punningly for 'wit'. The puns of this scene, lightly stressing the themes with which Jessica is involved, prepare for the gravity of the trial.
60–64   *suited ... Garnished.* A play on the fool's motley. It has been interpreted as a compliment to Will Kempe, who probably played Launcelot.
65   *Defy the matter* refuse to make sense (refuse to elucidate the matter)
      How cheer'st thou? How art thou?
77   *Pawned* staked, added

IV.1   (stage direction) *Enter the Duke, the magnificoes*. The
constitution and status of this court is ambiguous (see
Introduction, pp. 22–7). In the course of the scene the
law mutates from a Civil to a Criminal cause. In the
former case, Venice had a court of forty judges, for the
latter a similar composition but – until the fourteenth
century – presided over by the Doge. It is clear that
even if he knew the Venetian law, Shakespeare was not
concerned with 'realism'.

4   *stony adversary*. The scene opens with blatant partiality.

7   *qualify* moderate

13   *tyranny* violence (whether of emotion or of power over
a subject)

20–21   *strange . . . strange* unusual . . . unnatural

21   *apparent* clear, manifest

26   *moiety* portion (not necessarily a half, as *moitié*)

32   *Turks . . . Tartars* (again similar in import to the
categories of 'Jews, Turks, Infidels, and Heretics' in
the Good Friday Collect; see note to 1.3.108)

34   *gentle answer, Jew* (the climax of the punning on
'Gentile')

36   *holy Sabbath*. Shylock responds in kind to the Gentile
plea.

43   *my humour* my whim (or possibly a pun in the sense of
'witty caprice' and the fixed constitution of the Jon-
sonian 'humour')

46   *baned* poisoned

47   *gaping* (prepared for table, with fruit in its mouth)

49   *sings i'th'nose*. The bagpipe's drone, perhaps like the
whining, nasal voice of the Puritan.

50–51   *affection . . . passion*. Compare III.1.53–4: 'Hath not a
Jew . . . senses, affections, passions'; affections are
'desires', related to the will; passions are the emotions
associated with the affections; hence here 'Master of
passion'.

55   *necessary cat*. The cat is a domestic necessity to keep
down mice (this, with the adjective 'harmless' to

distinguish it from a cat which is a witch's familiar).

56   *woollen* covered with woollen cloth

60   *lodged* deep-seated
      certain fixed

62   *A losing suit* a suit involving inevitable material loss for
      Shylock. A moment of irony for the audience, anticipa-
      ting the *peripeteia* later in the scene by which Shylock
      is condemned to lose all.

70   *question* argue (a term of formal disputation)

76   *high-tops.* Compare the mast of I.1.28.

77   *fretten* fretted

88-9 *mercy . . . judgement* (a further anticipation of Shylock's
      reversal of fortune, and of the references to the Lord's
      Prayer in IV.1.198)

90-100 *You have among you many a purchased slave. . . .* This is
      the most intense expression of Shylock's desired power
      over Antonio; the 'pound of flesh' is the purchased life
      and Antonio a slave dearly bought to Shylock's will.

114-15 *tainted wether of the flock,* | *Meetest for death.* An
      interesting Gentile statement; in Jewish law a sacrificial
      beast had to be wholly unblemished.

114   *wether* ram

123   *sole . . . soul.* There is a parallel to this pun in *Romeo
      and Juliet*, I.4.14-15: 'You have dancing shoes | With
      nimble soles. I have a soul of lead' – but there is a still
      graver undertone in Gratiano's speech, anticipating
      Shylock's damnation.

125   *hangman's axe.* Compare *Measure for Measure*, IV.2.45-
      48: 'your hangman . . . your block and your axe'

128   *inexecrable.* The reading 'inexecrable' is found in the
      Qs and F1 and it was amended to 'inexorable' in F3.
      'Inexecrable' is an attractive reading ('cannot be suffi-
      ciently execrated') and it is paralleled by the line in
      Faustus 'thou damned witch and execrable dog'. While
      this parallel appears to make the Q reading certain,
      'inexorable' has also much to be said for it. The context
      relates to prayer ('can no prayers pierce thee?') and

'inexorable' may be read 'cannot be moved by prayer', from *orare*, to pray.

129 *And for thy life let justice be accused* and because of your very existence, let justice itself be brought into question

131 *Pythagoras.* He propounded the doctrine of the 'transmigration of souls'. Compare *Twelfth Night*, IV.2.49.

133-4 *currish ... wolf.* This is argued as a reference to the execution of Dr Lopez (*lupus* – wolf); see Introduction, p. 8.

167 *take your place.* Portia's status (like her precise location within the court) is ambiguous: is she a consultant to give 'counsel's opinion'; advocate for Antonio; or judge? If the last, her place, at the Duke's invitation, would be on the bench.

171 *Which is the merchant here? And which the Jew?* The relative dramatic significance of Antonio and Shylock has fluctuated in the published and stage history of the play. Lansdowne's adaptation is *The Jew of Venice* and by the nineteenth century Shylock was of such central significance that at his defeat at the end of this Act the play was frequently brought to a close.

177 *within his danger* in his power. A legal term expressed in the 'law French' *estre en son danger*; Old French *dangier*, absolute power. The word could also signify 'debt'.

181-202 *The quality of mercy ...* For Portia's speech see Introduction, pp. 25-7.

198 *that same prayer* the Lord's Prayer: 'forgive us our trespasses' or (in the Bishops' Bible) 'forgive us our debts as we forgive our debtors'. Note also the marginal note in the Geneva Bible, Matthew 6.12, of significance to the theme of *The Merchant of Venice*: 'They that forgive wrongs, to them sins are forgiven, but revenge is prepared for them that revenge' (see III.1.61-5, Shylock on Christian revenge).

200 *mitigate* moderate. But 'mercy' is part of the customary 'plea in mitigation' *after* guilt has been pronounced.

203   *My deeds upon my head.* If this reference be to the trial
of Christ (St Matthew 27.25, 'His blood be on us and
on our children'), Shylock has made its significance
sharper, taking the guilt solely to himself. Unlike
Launcelot in his reference to inherited guilt in III.5.1–2
(see note above) Shylock extends the pattern of references by assimilating the cry at Christ's trial ('on *us*
and on our children') to the teaching of Jeremiah 31
('They shall say no more. The fathers have eaten a sour
grape and the children's teeth are set on edge, for every
one·shall die for his own misdeeds'); Shylock here
assumes full personal responsibility for his pursuit of
Antonio's life.

215–16   *no power in Venice | Can alter a decree establishèd.* Laws
in Venice had the immutability attributed to those of
the Medes and Persians. See *Il Pecorone*: 'Venice was
a place where the law was enforced, and the Jew had
his rights fully and publicly.'

220   *Daniel.* Daniel was the young judge in the story of
Susannah and the Elders; he also detected the false
priest of Bel in Bel and the Dragon (both from the
Apocrypha); see Ezekiel 28.3: 'Behold, thou thinkest
thyself wiser than Daniel.' One might have expected
Shylock to have cited Solomon as the type of wise
judge and Lansdowne's version extends the reference:
'A *Daniel*, a *David*: So ripe in Wisdom And so young
in years! A second *Solomon*.' But Portia's 'youth' more
accords with Daniel than with Solomon.

225   *an oath in heaven* (taken with Tubal at the synagogue)
252   *balance* (known in Shakespeare's day in this plural form)
271–8   *Tell her the process of Antonio's end. . . .* A 'witty' speech
throughout: 'process' puns on 'manner' and 'legal
process'; Portia is in fact his 'judge' and an auditor of
his speech; 'all his heart' is precisely the penalty sought
by Shylock. This witty nonchalance (the quality of
sprezzatura cultivated by the courtier) was especially
to be shown at point of death. Lansdowne in a later,

less witty age, amplifies the pun to extinction: 'for I would have my Heart Seen by my Friend'.

293 *Barabbas.* He who 'for insurrection' was condemned to death and was released as an act of clemency at the Passover in place of Christ. The close association of the people's cry for Barabbas at the same time that they willed that Christ's blood be 'on us, and on our children' adds an ironic depth to this line in Shylock's mouth.

302 *Tarry a little.* Shakespeare dramatically points, with this verbal gesture, the precise moment of *peripeteia.*

303 *no jot of blood.* See Introduction, p. 24, for this denial of equity principles of which Shakespeare must have known.

326-7 *twentieth part | Of one poor scruple* (one grain by weight)

331 *on the hip.* See note to I.3.43.

346-54 *If it be proved against an alien . . .* These are the conditions which the Duke's mercy and Antonio's modify; see the note to IV.1.378.

373 *You take my life.* Compare Ecclesiasticus 34.23: 'Who so robbeth his neighbour of his living, doth as great sin as though he slew him to death.'

378 *quit the fine for.* It would seem that Shylock is treated with total clemency: his life is saved, Antonio holds one half of his property *in trust* for Jessica; and this ambiguous sentence must imply 'to quit (i.e. remit, settle – from *quietus*) the fine imposed of half his goods'. This was Lansdowne's reading: 'To quit the fine of one half of his goods.' Shylock therefore suffers no physical penalties – and in Lansdowne's play his enforced Christianity is omitted. (See Introduction, pp. 29-32.)

380 *in use.* A legal term, the device of 'a conveyance to user', whereby an estate intended for inheritance by a second person (Jessica in this instance) is made over to a third person (Antonio) for security of inheritance. In full legal terms, Antonio would be declared seised of half Shylock's estate to the use of Lorenzo and Jessica after Shylock's death.

384   *presently* forthwith

     become a Christian. Coryat declares of the Jews of Venice that 'all their goods are confiscated as soon as they embrace Christianity ... and so disclog their souls and consciences'. Shakespeare clearly excludes such an action and quotes the relevant scriptural text (line 373 above).

395   *godfathers* (a canting term for a jury)

401   *presently* without delay

403   *gratify* be courteous to, reward

409   *cope* give in recompense (? from Old English *ceapan*, to buy and sell, as in cheapen, Cheapside, Chipping Camden and chapman)

448   *commandèment* (a quadrisyllable here, though usually a trisyllable elsewhere in Shakespeare, except in *1 Henry VI*, I.3.20: 'From him I have express commandement')

452   *presently* at once

IV.2.15   *old swearing* ample oaths (a colloquial augmentative, paralleled by the Italian *vecchio* in the same sense; compare 'a high old time')

V.1   It has been customary to speak of the gracious lyricism of this opening to the fifth Act, a contrast to the sombre trial scene. In fact Shakespeare rarely indulges in such simple contrasts. This is no more an unflawed lyricism than the close of *A Midsummer Night's Dream* or the ironic opening of *Twelfth Night*. This playfulness of the lovers has sombre undertones in the literary parallels which they cite in their mock encounter: Troilus, Cressida, Thisbe, Dido, and Medea. This is then a 'flyting match', mocking the traditional devotees of love, such as those described in Chaucer's *Legend of Good Women*, the *Parliament of Fowls* and the *Knight's Tale*. These devotees of Venus were often illustrated in later medieval tapestries and manuscripts.

The first fourteen lines of the scene are indebted both to Chaucer and to Ovid's *Metamorphoses*, probably (as elsewhere in the play) in Golding's translation.

4-6 *Troilus . . . | Where Cressid lay.* Compare Chaucer, *Troilus and Criseyde*, V, 647-67.

7 *Thisbe.* Compare *A Midsummer Night's Dream*, V, and Chaucer, *Legend of Good Women*, 796-812.

10 *Dido with a willow in her hand.* From Chaucer's *Legend of Good Women* but more accurately reflecting the details of Ariadne's story than Dido's. The willow was a sign of forsaken love; see Desdemona's Willow Song and Spenser, *Faerie Queene*, I.1.9: 'worn of forlorn Paramours'. ·

13 *Medea.* Though she is associated with Thisbe and Dido in Chaucer, the gathering of herbs at full moon is from Ovid, *Metamorphoses*, VII; in Golding's translation, when the moon shone 'Most full of light', Medea 'gat her out of doors and wandered up and down'.

15-21 *steal . . . unthrift . . . Stealing her soul . . . ne'er a true [vow] . . . shrew.* These lines continue, despite the playfulness, the darker implications of the tragic lovers cited.

22 *Slander* (Jessica's previous speech, questioning Lorenzo's fidelity)

24 (stage direction) *Stephano.* The verse appears to demand the pronunciation Stepháno.

39 *Sola, sola!* Launcelot imitates the sound of a post horse as he gallops in.

46-7 *post . . . horn.* The post horn becomes a cornucopia in Launcelot's pun.

53 *music* (a consort of instruments, a small orchestra)

57 *Become* befit
touches phrases (derived from the touching or fingering the strings)

58 *floor of heaven* (both the sky and the overhanging canopy of the stage, painted with stars and heavenly signs)

59 *patens* (the dish, of silver or gold, from which the consecrated bread of the eucharist is served)

60–63 *There's not the smallest orb* . . . The music of the spheres
has been referred to many sources: the Pythagorean
doctrine of numbers and harmony which Wordsworth
echoes in *Ode on the Power of Sound*; Plato, *The Republic*,
X; nearer Shakespeare's day Montaigne, *On Custom*
(translated by Florio 1603), and, still nearer, Hooker,
Ecclesiastical Policy, V: 'Touching musical harmony . . .
such is the force thereof . . . that some have been
thereby induced to think that the soul itself by nature
is or hath in it harmony.' There may be also a scriptural
echo of Job, 38.7: 'Where wast thou when the morning
stars sang together?'

64 *muddy vesture.* The contrast between the soul and its
'muddy vesture' the body was a neo-platonic doctrine
familiar to Shakespeare and may be echoed in Hamlet's
longing for the dissolution of 'this too too solid [or
sullied] flesh'. Italian neo-platonism (which Shakespeare frequently echoes) carried the implications of
this doctrine still further in a complex mythology de-
picting the release of the soul from the body's bondage.
This could be depicted in religious form, for example in
the flaying of St Bartholomew, in Michelangelo's *Last
Judgement* in the Sistine Chapel; or in secular form in
the flaying of Marsyas by Apollo. (See Edgar Wind,
Pagan Mysteries in the Renaissance, 1958.)

66 *Diana* (as moon-goddess of chastity, appropriately in-
voked here)

79 *the poet* (Ovid)

81 *stockish* blockish, brutal

87 *Erebus* (a dark place on the way to Hades)

90–91 *candle . . . naughty world.* Compare St Matthew, 5.16:
'Let your light so shine before men that they may see
your good works . . .'

94 *A substitute shines brightly as a king* (a regular Shakespearian situation; compare Angelo in *Measure for
Measure* and Lorenzo as Portia's substitute in this play)

98 *your music.* Compare line 53 above.

99   *respect* comparison

109   *How the moon sleeps with Endymion.* If this refers to the two lovers, Lorenzo is identified with Endymion and Jessica with Diana who caused him to sleep on Latmos.

121   (stage direction) *tucket* a trumpet flourish (Italian *toccata*)

127–8   *We should hold day with the Antipodes | If you would walk in absence of the sun.* A puzzling speech, perhaps rightly explained by Malone: 'If you would always walk in the night, it would be day with us, as it now is on the other side of the globe.'

135–8   *bound ... acquitted.* It is characteristic of this final Act that the grave and even the potentially tragic themes of the play are punned on lightly.

144   *Would he were gelt* would he were a eunuch

148   *posy* an inscription on the inner surface of a ring, common in England in the seventeenth century. They were found also from classical times on the outside.

156   *respective* careful. Compare *Romeo and Juliet*, III.1.123: 'respective lenity'.

162   *scrubbèd* short. Warton suggested the emendation *stubbed*, since small birds were colloquially known as 'stubbed young ones'. But two instances from Philemon Holland's translation of Pliny's *Natural History* confirm Shakespeare's reading: 'Such will never prove fair trees, but shrubs only'; 'Verily a little scrubby plant it is, or shrub rather.'

199   *virtue* power (Latin *virtus*, Italian *virtù*). This was a term of some ambiguity in Shakespeare's day, rarely having moral overtones. Compare Tamburlaine's declaration that 'virtue solely is the sum of glory' with the gospel declaration that at the performance of a miracle Christ knew that 'virtue had gone out of him'. In the present passage, though the tone and the bantering echo of Bassanio's rhythms in Portia's reply keep the tension light, the 'virtue' of the ring reminds the playgoer of Shakespeare's later gravity over Desdemona's kerchief.

206   *ceremony* (a sacred symbol)

210   *civil doctor* (a pun on 'Doctor of Civil Law' and 'a courteous doctor')

230   *Argus* (the hundred-eyed)

237, 307 *clerk's pen . . . Nerissa's ring.* These two bawdy puns on the male and female sexual organs, both referred to Nerissa, maintain the prevailing tone of this Act, poised between romantic comedy and high seriousness.

244   *doubly sees himself.* A further light handling of the centrally serious theme of deceitful appearance; as applied by Portia to Bassanio it picks up lightly the motive of the casket scene.

251–2 *bound . . . soul . . . forfeit.* Antonio enters the witty exchange. The references to 'bond' and 'forfeit' are deepened by the middle term, 'soul', for in the former bond Antonio wagered no more than his flesh.

266   *grossly* licentiously

294   *manna.* The word comes appropriately (food in a desert place) after Portia's reference to 'Jessica' and 'rich Jew'. Shakespeare probably borrowed a pun here from the marginal glosses in the Geneva and Bishops' Bibles, which rounds off the Jewish element in the play. For in Exodus 16.15 ('They said every one to his neighbour, It is Manna') both Bibles refer in the margin to Manna (or 'Man') in the same terms: 'which signifieth a part, portion or gift'.

298   *upon inter'gatories.* It is characteristic that Portia's final speech should be in legal terms, a reference to the questioning of witnesses on oath.

The first known mention of Shakespeare's play is an entry on 22 July 1598 in the Stationers' Register of books authorized for publication. A printer called James Roberts entered 'a book of the Merchant of Venice, or otherwise called the Jew of Venice'. Two years later (1600) appeared 'The most excellent Historie of the *Merchant of Venice*. With the extreame crueltie of *Shylocke* the Iewe towards the sayd Merchant, in cutting a iust pound of his flesh: and the obtayning of *Portia* by the choyse of three chests. *As it hath beene diuers times acted by the Lord Chamberlaine his Seruants.* Written by William Shakespeare.' The title given on the first page of the text and in the running-titles at the top of each pair of pages is 'The comicall History of the Merchant of Venice'. We have no reason to suppose that these descriptions of the play are Shakespeare's; they sound more like the printer's inventions.

This first edition of the play (which we refer to as Q1) was printed probably from a manuscript that was close to Shakespeare's. It may have been his own rough manuscript which was kept as a working copy in the play-house. Two of the stage directions are in an imperative form ('open the letter', III.2.236; and 'play Musique', V.1.68) and perhaps indicate the closeness of the text to the play-house prompt-copy.

Q1 is our only authority for the text of the play. It was reprinted in 1619 by William Jaggard but the date of the original edition (1600) and the name of the original printer (James Roberts) were falsely kept on the title-page. This edition is referred to as Q2. It makes a few obvious corrections of errors in Q1, as well as introducing new errors of its own. The play was reprinted in the Folio edition of Shakespeare's plays in 1623. This is referred to as F. The printer of the Folio used Q1 as his copy; some corrections were made and some new errors

introduced. There is no reason to suppose that the changes in Q2
and in F had the author's approval; they were probably more or
less intelligent guesses made in the printing-house.

COLLATIONS

The following lists are *selective*. They include the more important and interesting variants. Minor changes which are not disputed, small variations in word-order, obvious misprints, and
grammatical corrections not affecting the sense, are not generally
included here. A few modernizations of spelling which sub-
stantially alter the form of the word are also included.

1

The following readings in the present text of *The Merchant of
Venice* are emendations of the words found in Q1 (which are
placed afterwards in the original spelling, with where appropriate the forms found in other early texts). A few of the alterations
were made in the printing of Q2 (1619), or in the folios F
(1623), F2 (1632), F3 (1663–4), F4 (1685). Most of the other
emendations were made by the eighteenth-century editors.

I.1.	13	curtsy] cursie Q1, Q2; curtsie F
	19	Peering] F; Piring Q1; Piering Q2
	27	Andrew docked] *Andrew* docks Q1, F; *Andrew* dockes Q2
	84	alabaster] Alablaster
I.2.	43	County Palatine] Q2; Countie Palentine Q1, F
	51–2	Le Bon] *Le Boune*
	56	Count Palatine] Q2; Count Palentine Q1, F
	57	throstle] Trassell Q1, Q2, F
I.3.	47	well-won] Q2; well-wone Q1; well-worne F
	75	compromised] compremyzd Q1, Q2; compremyz'd F
	131	breed of] F; breede for Q1, Q2
		barren] Q2; barraine Q1, F

II.1. 31 thee, lady] the Lady
       35 page] rage Q1, Q2, F
II.2.   3 (and elsewhere) Gobbo] Q2; Iobbe Q1, F
II.3. 11 did] F2; doe Q1, Q2, F
II.7. 69 *tombs*] *timber*
II.8. 39 Slubber] Q2, F; slumber
III.1. 27 fledged] Q2; flidge Q1; fledg'd F
       45 courtesy] cursie Q1; curtsie Q2, F
       97 Heard] heere
III.2. 67 eyes] F; eye
       81 vice] F2; voyce Q1; voice Q2, F
       93 make] maketh Q1, Q2; makes F
      101 Therefore thou] Therefore then thou
      204 roof] Q2; rough Q1, F
III.4. 49 Padua] Mantua
       50 cousin's hand] F; cosin hands Q1; Cosins hands
           Q2
       53 traject] Tranect Q1, Q2, F
       79 for a wife] for wife
III.5. 20 e'en] Q2, F; in Q1
     72-3 merit it, | In] meane it, it | in Q1; meane it,
           then | In Q2; meane it, it | In F
IV.1. 30 his state] Q2, F; this states Q1
       51 Master] Maisters Q1, Q2; Masters F
       74 bleat] F; bleake Q1, Q2
       75 mountain] mountaine of
      100 'tis] Q2, F; as Q1
      150 CLERK] *not in* Q1, Q2, F *and so presumably attri-*
           buted to the Duke
V.1.   49 Sweet soul] *as the last words of Launcelot's previous*
           speech in Q1, Q2, F
       51 Stephano] Q2; *Stephen* Q1, F
      233 my] Q2, F; mine Q1

2

The following are some of the more interesting and important
variant readings and proposed emendations *not* accepted in the

present text of *The Merchant of Venice*. Many of these rejected readings will be found in older editions (especially of the nineteenth century).

The reading of this edition (which derives from Q1 unless otherwise stated) is given first, followed by the rejected variants. If a source of the variant is not given, the reading is an emendation by an editor (most of them are of the eighteenth century).

I.1. 10   on] of

I.2. 6–7   mean happiness] smal happinesse F

   30–31   one who you shall] one who shall Q2, F

     72   Scottish] Q1, Q2; other F

I.3.22–3   water thieves and land thieves] land thieves and water thieves

     62   ye would] he would haue Q2; he would F; we would

I.3. 131   barren] bearing

II.1. 18   wit] will

     35   page] rage Q1, Q2, F; rogue (C. J. Sisson); wag (J. Dover Wilson)

II.2.155–6 the twinkling] the twinkling of an eye Q2

II.4. 5   us] as F4

II.6. 14   younger] younker

II.9. 78   wroth] wroath Q1, Q2, F; wrath, ruth, roth (=ruth)

III.1. 97   Heard] heere Q1; here; where?

III.2. 106   paleness] plainness

   158   sum of something] sum of nothing F

IV.1. 56   woollen] wauling

   128   inexecrable] inexorable F3

   150   CLERK] *not in* Q1, Q2, F; NERISSA (C. J. Sisson)

   256   Is it so] It is not F

V.1.41–2   Master Lorenzo? Master Lorenzo!] M. Lorenzo, & M. Lorenzo Q1; Master Lorenzo and Mistress Lorenzo?

   109   Peace! (*Music ceases*) How] Peace, how Q1; Peace, ho!

Stage Directions

The stage directions of the present edition are based on those of the quartos of 1600 and 1619, and the first Folio. Some of the original directions have simply been regularized. For instance, at the beginning of II.2 the Quarto's '*Enter the Clowne alone*' has been altered to '*Enter Launcelot Gobbo, alone*'. Similarly, instructions for actions obviously demanded by the text have been added: '*He looks at his palm*' (II.2.146) is an instance. When the quarto text was reprinted in the Folio the principal changes in the stage directions were of additional directions for flourishes of cornets. These have been incorporated. The following list includes the more interesting changes from the first Quarto. Q1 refers to the Quarto of 1600; Q2 to that of 1619; Q indicates both quartos; and F refers to the first Folio, of 1623.

II.1.	0	*Flourish of cornets* is not in Q ; F has *Flo. Cornets.*
	46	*Exeunt* Q ; *Cornets. Exeunt.* F
II.2.	72	not in Q , F
	104	*Enter* Bassanio *with a follower or two.* Q , F
	108	Q2; not in Q1, F
	156	*Exit Clowne.* Q , F
II.4.	9	*with a Letter* F; not in Q
II.6.	25	*Iessica* aboue. Q , F
	50	not in Q , F
	57	Enter *Iessica.* Q , F
	59	*Exit.* Q , F
II.7.0, 77		*Flourish of cornets* is not in Q . F has *Flo. Cornets.* after *Enter Salarino and Solanio* (II.8.0). Probably this was accidentally misplaced from II.7.77. It seems likely that Morocco's entry as well as his exit would have been signalled by a flourish.
II.9.	3	*Flourish of cornets* is not in Q ; F has *Flor. Cornets.*
	78	not in Q , F
III.3.	0	For *Solanio* Q1 has *Salerio*, and Q2 *Salarino*. F has *Solanio*.
IV.1.	0	*Salerio* and *with others* are not in Q , F

118   *dressed like a Lawyer's Clerk* is not in Q , F
120   not in Q , F
IV.1. 163   *dressed like a Doctor of Laws* is not in Q , F
423   not in Q , F
IV.2.   0   *Enter Nerrissa.* Q ; *Enter Portia and Nerrissa.* F
V.1. 65   not in Q , F
109   F ; not in Q
121   F ; not in Q

Discover more about our forthcoming books through Penguin's FREE newspaper...

Penguin
Quarterly

It's packed with:

- exciting features
- author interviews
- previews & reviews

books from your favourite
films & TV series

exclusive competitions
& much, much more...

Write off for your free copy today to:
Dept JC
Penguin Books Ltd
FREEPOST
West Drayton
Middlesex
UB7 0BR
NO STAMP REQUIRED

FOR THE BEST IN PAPERBACKS, LOOK FOR THE 🐧

In every corner of the world, on every subject under the sun, Penguin represents quality and variety -- the very best in publishing today.

For complete information about books available from Penguin – including Puffins, Penguin Classics and Arkana – and how to order them, write to us at the appropriate address below. Please note that for copyright reasons the selection of books varies from country to country.

In the United Kingdom: Please write to *Dept JC, Penguin Books Ltd, FREEPOST, West Drayton, Middlesex, UB7 0BR.*

If you have any difficulty in obtaining a title, please send your order with the correct money, plus ten per cent for postage and packaging, to *PO Box No 11, West Drayton, Middlesex*

In the United States: Please write to *Dept BA, Penguin, 299 Murray Hill Parkway, East Rutherford, New Jersey 07073*

In Canada: Please write to *Penguin Books Canada Ltd, 2801 John Street, Markham, Ontario L3R 1B4*

In Australia: Please write to the *Marketing Department, Penguin Books Australia Ltd, P.O. Box 257, Ringwood, Victoria 3134*

In New Zealand: Please write to the *Marketing Department, Penguin Books (NZ) Ltd, Private Bag, Takapuna, Auckland 9*

In India: Please write to *Penguin Overseas Ltd, 706 Eros Apartments, 56 Nehru Place, New Delhi, 110019*

In the Netherlands: Please write to *Penguin Books Netherlands B.V., Postbus 3507, NL–1001 AH, Amsterdam*

In West Germany: Please write to *Penguin Books Ltd, Friedrichstrasse 10–12, D–6000 Frankfurt/Main 1*

In Spain: Please write to *Alhambra Longman S.A., Fernandez de la Hoz 9, E–28010 Madrid*

In Italy: Please write to *Penguin Italia s.r.l., Via Como 4, I-20096 Pioltello (Milano)*

In France: Please write to *Penguin France S.A., 17 rue Lejeune, F-31000 Toulouse*

In Japan: Please write to *Longman Penguin Japan Co Ltd, Yamaguchi Building, 2–12–9 Kanda Jimbocho, Chiyoda-Ku, Tokyo 101*

The Royal Shakespeare Company today is probably one of the best known theatre companies in the world, playing regularly to audiences of more than a million people a year. The RSC has three theatres in Stratford-upon-Avon, the Royal Shakespeare Theatre, the Swan Theatre and The Other Place, and two theatres in London's Barbican Centre, the Barbican Theatre and The Pit. The Company also has an annual season in Newcastle-upon-Tyne and regularly undertakes tours throughout the UK and overseas.

Find out more about the RSC and its current repertoire by joining the Company's mailing list. Not only will you receive advance information of all the Company's activities, but also priority booking, special ticket offers, copies of the RSC Magazine and special offers on RSC publications and merchandise.

If you would like to receive details of the Company's work and an application form for the mailing list please write to:

RSC Membership Office
Royal Shakespeare Theatre
FREEPOST
Stratford-upon-Avon
CV37 6BR

or telephone: 0789 205301

FOR THE BEST IN PAPERBACKS, LOOK FOR THE 🐧

PENGUIN CRITICAL STUDIES

Described by *The Times Educational Supplement* as 'admirable' and 'superb', Penguin Critical Studies is a specially developed series of critical essays on the major works of literature for use by students in universities, colleges and schools.

titles published or in preparation include:

SHAKESPEARE
Antony and Cleopatra
As You Like It
Hamlet
Julius Caesar
King Lear
Measure for Measure
A Midsummer Night's Dream
Much Ado About Nothing
Othello
Romeo and Juliet
Shakespeare's History Plays
Shakespeare – Text into Performance
The Tempest
Troilus and Cressida
The Winter's Tale

CHAUCER
Chaucer
The Nun's Priest's Tale
The Pardoner's Tale
The Prologue to the Canterbury
   Tales

NEW PENGUIN SHAKESPEARE

General Editor: T. J. B. Spencer

All's Well That Ends Well Barbara Everett
Antony and Cleopatra Emrys Jones
As You Like It H. J. Oliver
The Comedy of Errors Stanley Wells
Coriolanus G. R. Hibbard
Hamlet T. J. B. Spencer
Henry IV, Part 1 P. H. Davison
Henry IV, Part 2 P. H. Davison
Henry V A. R. Humphreys
Henry VI, Part 1 Norman Sanders
Henry VI, Part 2 Norman Sanders
Henry VI, Part 3 Norman Sanders
Henry VIII A. R. Humphreys
Julius Caesar Norman Sanders
King John R. L. Smallwood
King Lear G. K. Hunter
Love's Labour's Lost John Kerrigan
Macbeth G. K. Hunter
Measure for Measure J. M. Nosworthy
The Merchant of Venice W. Moelwyn Merchant
The Merry Wives of Windsor G. R. Hibbard
A Midsummer Night's Dream Stanley Wells
Much Ado About Nothing R. A. Foakes
The Narrative Poems Maurice Evans
Othello Kenneth Muir
Pericles Philip Edwards
Richard II Stanley Wells
Richard III E. A. J. Honigmann
Romeo and Juliet T. J. B. Spencer
The Sonnets and *A Lover's Complaint* John Kerrigan
The Taming of the Shrew G. R. Hibbard
The Tempest Anne Righter (Anne Barton)
Timon of Athens G. R. Hibbard
Troilus and Cressida R. A. Foakes
Twelfth Night M. M. Mahood
The Two Gentlemen of Verona Norman Sanders
The Two Noble Kinsmen N. W. Bawcutt
The Winter's Tale Ernest Schanzer